THE SILENCE OF THE SPIRITS

GLOBAL AFRICAN VOICES
Dominic Thomas, editor

I Was an Elephant Salesman: Adventures between Dakar, Paris, and Milan
Pap Khouma, Edited by Oreste Pivetta
Translated by Rebecca Hopkins
Introduction by Graziella Parati

Little Mother: A Novel
Cristina Ali Farah
Translated by Giovanna Bellesia-Contuzzi and Victoria Offredi Poletto
Introduction by Alessandra Di Maio

Life and a Half: A Novel
Sony Labou Tansi
Translated by Alison Dundy
Introduction by Dominic Thomas

Transit: A Novel
Abdourahman A. Waberi
Translated by David Ball and Nicole Ball

Cruel City: A Novel
Mongo Beti
Translated by Pim Higginson

Blue White Red: A Novel
Alain Mabanckou
Translated by Alison Dundy

The Past Ahead: A Novel
Gilbert Gatore
Translated by Marjolijn de Jager

Queen of Flowers and Pearls: A Novel
Gabriella Ghermandi
Translated by Giovanna Bellesia-Contuzzi and Victoria Offredi Poletto

The Shameful State: A Novel
Sony Labou Tansi
Translated by Dominic Thomas
Foreword by Alain Mabanckou

Kaveena
Boubacar Boris Diop
Translated by Bhakti Shringarpure and Sara C. Hanaburgh

Murambi, The Book of Bones
Boubacar Boris Diop
Translated by Fiona Mc Laughlin

The Heart of the Leopard Children
Wilfried N'Sondé
Translated by Karen Lindo

Harvest of Skulls
Abdourahman A. Waberi
Translated by Dominic Thomas

Jazz and Palm Wine
Emmanuel Dongala
Translated by Dominic Thomas

THE SILENCE
OF THE SPIRITS

WILFRIED N'SONDÉ

Translated by KAREN LINDO

INDIANA UNIVERSITY PRESS

This book is a publication of

Indiana University Press
Office of Scholarly Publishing
Herman B Wells Library 350
1320 East 10th Street
Bloomington, Indiana 47405 USA

iupress.indiana.edu

Original publication in French as
Le Silence des esprits
© 2010 Actes Sud
English translation © 2017 by Indiana
University Press

Manufactured in the United States of
America

Library of Congress Cataloging-
in-Publication Data

Names: N'Sondé, Wilfried, author. |
Lindo, Karen, translator.
Title: The silence of the spirits /
Wilfried N'Sondé ; translated by
Karen Lindo.
Other titles: Silence des esprits.
English | Global African voices.
Description: Bloomington, Ind. :
Indiana University Press, 2017. |
Series: Global African voices |
"Original publication in French as
Le Silence des esprits (c) 2010
Actes Sud." | Includes biblio-
graphical references.
Identifiers: LCCN 2017008799
(print) | LCCN 2017009714
(ebook) | ISBN 9780253028945
(pbk. : alk. paper) | ISBN
9780253029072 (e-book)
Subjects: LCSH: Africans—
France—Fiction. | Illegal
aliens—France—Fiction.
Classification: LCC PQ 3989.3.N76
S5513 2017 (print) | LCC
PQ 3989.3.N76 (ebook) | DDC
843.92—dc23
LC record available at https://lccn.
loc.gov/2017008799

1 2 3 4 5 22 21 20 19 18 17

To Paul N'Sondé . . . and other martyrs

Because it is not enough to live, you must
also be beautiful!

SERGE MNSA N'SONDÉ

And then he brought another horse, red. Whoever
mounted it received the power to remove peace from
earth, so that men could cut each other's throats.

APOCALYPSE, VI, 4

The moon had flowered from my green chrysanthemums
When the wolves secretly recited anathema.
In the lowlands, requiems are the rage.
A weary prayer pronounced like a presage:

Cain today is armed with an axe,
In a cowardly gesture, he has again struck,
He spits out like a vampire his lifeless victim
Then tramples on the rhymes that yesterday I had gathered!

My body goes out beneath his sad smile
To escape mornings that terrify and cause suffering.

Cain today is armed with an axe,
In a cowardly gesture, he has again struck.

My mother had woven my shroud of diamonds
Because injured too often my heart bled a long time!

He spits out like a vampire his lifeless victim
Then tramples on the rhymes that yesterday I had gathered.

SARTRE WILFRIED PARACLET N'SONDÉ

CONTENTS

XIII

Foreword / Dominic Thomas

1

The Silence of the Spirits

FOREWORD

"The Silence of the Spirits:
From Civil Conflict to the War of Identities"

> *Meeting is only the beginning of separation.*
>
> Japanese Buddhist proverb

Following *Le cœur des enfants léopards* (2007), published in the Global African Voices series as *The Heart of the Leopard Children* in 2016, *The Silence of the Spirits*, initially published in French as *Le silence des esprits* in 2010, is Wilfried N'Sondé's second novel. Born in Brazzaville in the Republic of the Congo, N'Sondé grew up in France. His work examines various facets of the postcolonial condition, the tenuous relationship between Africa and Europe, the post-migratory experience, and the challenges of belonging and integration. However, the pioneering spirit of his work stands out when he turns his attention to the multiple ways in which individuals negotiate identities and relationships in France, a country that has attempted to foreclose the colonial past without fully thinking it through or for that matter finding a path to addressing this historical legacy and its multicultural realities. As N'Sondé has claimed, the result has been the inevitable introduction of "questionable criteria in order to divide and categorize, driving us gradually further away from the essence of being and magic of words."[1] This unwillingness to consider how the past ultimately continues to shape the future has introduced an awkward silence, one that is "not silence as in secret," as Srilata Ravi has shown, "but silence as in language, . . . and as such becomes the shared space where cosmopolitanism as intelligence, curiosity and a challenge can operate. As both reason and affect, N'Sondé's silence as communion is a metaphor for the practice of conversation, one that does not define itself as failed or completed. Cosmopolitanism as conversation does not end—hence it poses the challenge of continued engagement."[2]

Even though the French Republic remains "one and indivisible" as enshrined in the first constitution of 1791, a principle that underscores the commitment to protecting the rights of all citizens regardless of ethnicity, religion, or other social associations, the fact remains that the equality of citizens simply does not exist. To this end, N'Sondé's own background has always meant, even though in principle this should not be a factor, that, "depending on the context," as Myriam Louviot has observed, "the author is considered either African or French, a spokesperson of sorts on issues of diversity."[3] Not surprisingly, N'Sondé has him-

1. Wilfried N'Sondé, "Ethnidentité," in *Je est un autre: Pour une identité-monde*, edited by Michel Le Bris and Jean Rouaud (Paris: Gallimard, 2010), 100.

2. Srilata Ravi, "Toward an Afropean Cosmopolitanism: Hospitality, Friendship and the African Immigrant," in *Francophone Afropean Literatures*, edited by Nicki Hitchcott and Dominic Thomas (Liverpool: Liverpool University Press, 2014), 140.

3. Myriam Louviot, "Parcours d'un roman postcolonial francophone en France et en Allemagne: *Le Cœur des enfants léopards* de Wilfried N'Sondé," *Trajectoires*, December 15, 2010, http://trajectoires.revues.org/589.

self repeatedly commented on this question: "What is the point of me getting hoarse from explaining who I am or who I would like to be? There is nothing I can do. My thoughts are being kept in check. My words have no meaning. They believe they have summarized my ideas intelligently by reducing me to a series of nostalgic and exotic images, filled with a mixture of compassion and guilt, all well-intentioned. A romantic sketch, inherited from colonial haze and archaic prejudices."[4] How then has a novel such as *The Silence of the Spirits* been able to simultaneously explore such complex twenty-first-century issues while also advancing the conversation in meaningful ways?

After a long day at a Paris hospital where she works as a nurse's aid, Christelle finally heads home on the regional commuter train. Daydreaming, dozing off, this young French woman's focus eventually settles on the passenger facing her, a young man named Clovis Nzila. He is clearly distressed, out of place, and the reader learns that he is in fact a former African child soldier who has ended up in France as a *sans-papiers*, an illegal, undocumented migrant. As French psychoanalyst Charles Baudoin once wrote, "Nothing predisposes to fear like the conviction that we shall be afraid, and, above all, the conviction that we shall be afraid in certain specific conditions."[5] Somewhat unexpectedly then, Christelle reaches out to him, and these two passengers who otherwise might never have met find themselves on the same train, in a space in which time is temporarily interrupted,

4. Wilfried N'Sondé, "Francastérix," in *Francophone Afropean Literatures*, edited by Nicki Hitchcott and Dominic Thomas, translated by Karen Lindo (Liverpool: Liverpool University Press, 2014), 209.

5. Charles Baudoin, *Suggestion and Autosuggestion: A Psychological and Pedagogical Study Based on the Investigations Made by the New Nancy School*, translated by Eden Paul and Cedar Paul (New York: Dodd, Mead and Company, 1921), 70.

suspended long enough for a metaphorical and physical journey of discovery toward the other to begin.

On the surface, they have little in common, but N'Sondé gradually discloses information about them that will provide the coordinates of their relationship, the circumstances in which discovery and openness to the other becomes conceivable. "Like mine," Nzila realizes, "her heart had been broken during her childhood, a nightmare that haunts her and works on her behind her veil of oblivion even to this day. The shadows of her stepfather's hands and gaze on her bare thighs. All the years of feeling defiled. A bitter wound in her stomach, a hideous scar covering the memory of it all." We learn that, now living alone in a small apartment, she was molested as a child and was later the victim of domestic abuse at the hands of an alcoholic husband. As for Nzila, "Every day, I kept a low profile in Paris, walking with my head down and staring at my feet to avoid looking in front of me. I'd forgotten all about the dream, which risked ending up in bureaucracy, a file with some numbers stamped on it. I was running away, heading nowhere, to avoid being detained, enclosed behind bars, with wrists and ankles handcuffed, accused of having tried everything, defied every unimaginable danger, flirted with death a thousand times, suffered everyone's contempt, and all I wanted was simply to live!" A shared history of violence brings them together, but their hybridity threatens the social order, the monolithism of a society in which difference has no place, yet in which those very differences structure and define social relations. In her professional environment, Christelle "was about making others happy," and rather than be governed by fear, her impulse is instead to humanize those whose paths (it is worth noting that in Kikongo, for example, *nzila* means a passage, a path or a way) she crosses: "She'd forgotten her own worries, escaped from her own labyrinth of anxieties and boredom to take care of me, an illegal immigrant, far more destitute than she."

Christelle's decision to extend a helping hand to Nzila, to provide him with a place to stay, a shelter, serves to address broader societal circumstances. In 2009, and therefore at the time of writing *The Silence of the Spirits*, the question of providing assistance to *sans-papiers* and refugees was being reviewed in the French parliament and was a hotly debated and divisive issue. Already back in 2003, several campaigns had been launched against laws that defined the degree to which individuals, associations, or organizations could provide assistance or help to illegal or undocumented foreigners, according to which "anyone who, directly or indirectly, helps, facilitates or tries to facilitate the entry, the circulation or the unlawful residence of a foreigner in France" could be subject to prosecution. Thus, in the face of increased government control and restrictions over immigration and the accompanying debasing and dehumanizing logic shaping such initiatives and measures, a term was adopted to designate those attempts at criminalizing such efforts, namely a *délit d'hospitalité*, or "offense of solidarity." N'Sondé's staging of hospitality, of the precarious position in which such choices place citizens, and the criminalizing of the implied intimacy, therefore shapes much of the narrative.

In the eighteenth century, in the famous *Encyclopédie*, one could read under the entry for "hospitality" that "I define this virtue as a liberality exercised towards foreigners, especially if one receives them into one's home: the just measure of this type of beneficence depends on what contributes the most to the great end that men must have as a goal, namely reciprocal help, fidelity, exchange between various states, concord, and the duties of the members of a shared civil society."[6] Christelle's predisposition

6. Chevalier Louis de Jaucourt, "Hospitality," in *The Encyclopedia of Diderot & d'Alembert Collaborative Translation Project*, translated by Sophie Bourgault (Ann Arbor: Michigan Publishing, University of

to care for others professionally may therefore be commendable, "Sentimental by nature, Christelle was always sensitive to those who cried out and asked for help," but her decision to extend this hospitality into the private realm ends up being very much at odds with the broader inhospitable environment in France. This is especially true when one considers, as the novel does, the prevailing actions of the authorities and their representatives, eager to demonstrate their effectiveness at enforcing and protecting a social order that has grown intolerant and suspicious of outsiders and elected to embrace racial profiling, police controls, and ID checks.

From a much longer colonial and postcolonial history—defined by interconnections, neocolonial policies, globalization—two individuals, abandoned, orphaned, unwanted, rejected, and even cursed, somehow find refuge, the courage to risk intimacy. "I was so proud that she'd chosen me," Nzila shares with the reader. "We were slipping into the craziness of love. Christelle and me, we'd connected. She'd brought me into her universe. Her words gave me hope and enveloped me in an aura of light in the solitary night." As Karen Lindo has shown, "The physical abandon in which they give themselves over to the pleasures of the body enables the couple to take refuge, however short-lived, from the abuse that has heretofore marked their individual trajectories."[7] However, as Lindo goes on to ask, "Who are the young characters that people N'Sondé's novels? What are their values and how does

Michigan Library, 2013), http://hdl.handle.net/2027/spo.did2222.0002.761 (accessed April 14, 2016). Originally published as "Hospitalité," in *Encyclopédie ou Dictionnaire raisonné des sciences, des arts et des métiers*, volume 8 (Paris, 1765), 314.

7. Karen Lindo, "N'Sondé Post-2005 Youth Mural: Exploring Afro-Europe in Wilfried N'Sondé's Literary Landscape," in *Afroeuropean Cartographies*, edited by Dominic Thomas (Newcastle upon Tyne: Cambridge Scholars Publishing, 2014), 119.

this heterogeneous population manifest its sufferings and its aspirations?"[8] Nzila has been driven out of his native village, moved up from street urchin to a role in an "army" in which his zealous engagement has provided him for a while with a distorted sense of meaning and even an identity. He may now appear on a Paris commuter train as a frightened, vulnerable migrant, but "I was dragging my disaster along with me like a ball and chain. Impossible for me to turn my back on the past and make that big break and advance toward new possibilities, the hope for a life of stars, happiness." N'Sondé's novel therefore provides, through the safe haven Christelle offers, a space in which his story can be recounted, the violent atrocities accounted for and named, such that the process of historical reckoning can begin: "I'd have given anything to forget and for her to never know what I'd really done. Her eyes beseeched me. Couldn't she simply think about the present and build a future with me? Christelle wanted to know everything, every last detail of that period of my life, the truth. I was asking her to appreciate the new man that she was going to make of me, but the questions were going around in her mouth, in her eyes, kept cascading down!"

N'Sondé demands our presence as readers and listeners, enlists us in the broader process of testimony. How will Christelle react, what is at stake in assuming responsibility, acknowledging transgression, and how will we, as readers, position ourselves? How can a relationship survive confession? What are the limits of empathy, of forgiveness? How does one archive knowledge, restore humanity, and ultimately achieve reconciliation? N'Sondé thus presents us with two societies that continue to struggle with the process of fostering inclusive modes of coexistence, and in which violence and ethnic and identity conflict persist. As Myriam Louviot has argued, N'Sondé's work confronts the

8. Ibid., 116.

"translinguistic and cultural dimension of postcolonial problems," and "much could be gained from comparing the writings of authors such as Wilfried N'Sondé with those of other European migrants."[9] Indeed, from his own experiences, N'Sondé has written of how he "realized that the decision to come to Germany had allowed me to finally distance myself from a kind of hexagonal schizophrenia: that of being at once a French citizen whose equal rights were clearly and loudly affirmed but yet whose skin color gave rise to such great rants and ravings that I became increasingly skeptical of what was still being taught at university. Only too accustomed to police checks and the standard disregard for formalities and the patronizing use of the familiar 'tu', I quickly had to learn to answer their stupid questions and accept the humiliation if only to avoid a more serious incident. I soon came to realize that this recurrent police harassment was inversely proportionate to the whiteness of one's complexion."[10] In a country in which the "Frenchness" of non-white individuals has today, once again, become suspect, and the eventuality of stripping "bi-nationals" of their "French" nationality been invoked, Salman Rushdie's notion of "double unbelonging" has gained additional credence.[11]

The passage, path, or way to the other requires courage, a sense of adventure, but primarily moral imagination. N'Sondé's poetic musicality is enchanting but also disquieting, haunting, and unsettling. In the words of the great South African writer Antjie Krog, "To be vulnerable is to be fully human. It's the only way you can bleed into other people."[12]

9. Louviot, "Parcours d'un roman postcolonial francophone en France et en Allemagne."
10. N'Sondé, "Francastérix," 204.
11. Salman Rushdie, *East, West* (London: Jonathan Cape, 1994), 141.
12. Unpublished interview with Denis Hirson, 1995.

BIBLIOGRAPHY

Baudoin, Charles. *Suggestion and Autosuggestion: A Psychological and Pedagogical Study Based on the Investigations Made by the New Nancy School.* Translated by Eden Paul and Cedar Paul. New York: Dodd, Mead and Company, 1921.

Bragard, Véronique. "Parisian Alternative Cartographies: Meandering the Ambivalent Banlieue in Wilfried N'Sondé's Fiction." In *Metropolitan Mosaics and Melting-Pots: Paris and Montreal in Francophone Literatures,* edited by Pascale De Souza and Adlai Murdoch, 135–155. Newcastle upon Tyne: Cambridge Scholars Publishing, 2013.

Jaucourt, Chevalier Louis de. "Hospitality." In *The Encyclopedia of Diderot & d'Alembert Collaborative Translation Project.* Translated by Sophie Bourgault. Ann Arbor: Michigan Publishing, University of Michigan Library, 2013. http://hdl.handle.net/2027/spo.did2222.0002.761 (accessed April 14, 2016). Originally published as "Hospitalité," in *Encyclopédie ou Dictionnaire raisonné des sciences, des arts et des métiers,* volume 8, 314 (Paris, 1765).

Lindo, Karen. "N'Sondé Post-2005 Youth Mural: Exploring Afro-Europe in Wilfried N'Sondé's Literary Landscape." In *Afroeuropean Cartographies,* edited by Dominic Thomas, 112–131. Newcastle upon Tyne: Cambridge Scholars Publishing, 2014.

Louviot, Myriam. "Parcours d'un roman postcolonial francophone en France et en Allemagne: *Le Cœur des enfants léopards* de Wilfried N'Sondé." *Trajectoires,* December 15, 2010, http://trajectoires.revues.org/589.

N'Sondé, Wilfried. "Ethnidentité." In *Je est un autre: Pour une identité-monde,* edited by Michel Le Bris and Jean Rouaud, 95–100. Paris: Gallimard, 2010.

———. "Francastérix." Translated by Karen Lindo. In *Francophone Afropean Literatures,* edited by Nicki Hitchcott and Dominic Thomas, 203–210. Liverpool: Liverpool University Press, 2014.

Ravi, Srilata. "Toward an Afropean Cosmopolitanism: Hospitality, Friendship and the African Immigrant." In *Francophone Afropean Literatures,* edited by Nicki Hitchcott and Dominic Thomas, 138–154. Liverpool: Liverpool University Press, 2014.

Rushdie, Salman. *East, West.* London: Jonathan Cape, 1994.

THE SILENCE OF THE SPIRITS

MARCELLINE TOOK ME by the hand and lay down next to me. Once again we were fused. She took her time to tell me her story. I listened attentively and cried while kissing her hands because the traumas of war and the endless disillusionments had definitively shattered her dreams for happiness. All these disappointments had undermined her trust in humanity. My sister had decided to live in a holding pattern, as a recluse, and limit her interactions to the bare minimum.

During these periods of solitude, she implored Mother Earth, the temperamental Majesty that had created all that we see and that we cannot see in this world, to find me again, the only glimmer of joy and purity that remained anchored in her memory. The goddess's benevolence had made it possible for her to visit my spirit. Once she had unburdened herself, she was finally able to feel relieved, and with a smile on her face, Marcelline let me go, leaving behind a vague feeling of sensual pleasure on my shoulder. Bitterness too. Because she had survived at the expense of her body and soul.

I WOKE UP, weighed down by my sister's story, confused, with a faint image of her, smiling, radiant, more beautiful and happier than ever. Her silhouette gradually disappeared into a mist.

When the mist before my eyes had dissipated, I recognized Christelle's body beside me. Together, we were bathed in the warmth and bright red daylight gradually increasing, filtered by the curtains. Half naked, she lay on my torso, both of us stretched out beneath a beautiful disorder of white sheets, clothing, hastily removed the night before, now scattered about, our legs intertwined in a delicate touch.

Her full head of red and silver hair flowed off the pillow we were sharing and spread out lightly across my chest and belly. I was surprised to see her fingers wrapped around my arms. Even while she was sleeping, she had entwined herself with me. Christelle must have been holding me like this for most of the night.

Her head had melted perfectly into the curved angle of my shoulder and neck. Her thick, wavy mane of hair hid my face a little. She let herself go, relaxed and slept, serene. Watching her filled me with that ineffable feeling of peace and warmth that I had discovered while lying beside her.

I could not get enough of her milky white skin, with freckles that had blended in with other spots that had come in over time. I watched the slow and steady movement of her breathing through her nose. I was amazed at how our night of love together had left her feeling so carefree.

Christelle was snoozing. I clumsily ventured a hand into the depths near her hips, a timid journey toward the tender part of her belly, into the small of her back, to the territory beneath a thin, soft, transparent duvet that awakened from my caresses. Christelle quivered and sighed deeply. Careful not to offend me, she gently removed my fingers, once they made their way toward the moist mystery just above her thighs.

"I'm good like this—come closer, come next to me!"

~

She had murmured the words in a whisper. Lovingly, Christelle pressed a wet kiss on my mouth and another one in the palm of my hand, which she delicately placed between the mattress and her warm breast. My lover turned toward me and gave a hint of a smile. She pulled me into her movement so that her back gradually married perfectly the shape of my belly.

~

From the sofa bed where we had our first embrace rose a languorous dance of warm, moist scents, perfumes of stirred senses, colorful fragrances, an irresistible magic that rekindled our desires.

Relaxed, feeling free in my embrace, she fell asleep again. I touched her silky shoulder with my lips and the tip of my tongue. I will be her brother and her guardian. I will redeem the errors of my ways thanks to our shared happiness! Christelle kept her eyes closed, and the rounded, prominent curves of her body pressed against my skin. Amid all the tenderness after all that intensity, I felt unburdened, and I sighed too, promising to always watch over her so that she will never have to suffer!

~

After our frantic, painful lives, Christelle and I were learning to relax. We were taking a break to take care of each other's wounds. Two loners, still cautious, kissing and touching each other, offering a hand to each other. Hope, a kind of intoxicating giddiness, had given our tragedies a run for their money and was beginning to feel like love.

CHRISTELLE HAD TAKEN me in by chance during a suburban train ride. She admitted to having rescued me out of compassion as you might do for a wounded animal suffering on the roadside. She had forgotten her own worries, escaped from her own labyrinth of anxieties and boredom to take care of me, an illegal immigrant, far more destitute than she.

After her shift had ended on the day we met, she had rushed and taken a quick shower, dressed quickly so that she would not miss the bus. She arrived out of breath, but it had been too late. Disappointed, she decided to head to the train station on foot, enjoy a little walk and take advantage of the afternoon. After all, what was the rush? No one was waiting for her at home. She strolled along the Boulevard de l'Hôpital, congested with pedestrians and cars. As she was crossing the Pont d'Austerlitz, she saw me for the first time. She was immediately moved by my deep sad expression. Christelle thought I might have been lost in a dream. With my fist beneath my chin, I was peering at all the frozen garbage being carried along by the Seine on that February day. Christelle saw me as a man alone in the middle of nowhere, cowering into his skin, wishing his head would disappear into his shoulders. Today, when she remembers how poorly I was dressed, she smiles. She had felt an incredible sadness for me.

～

Christelle casually continued on her way to Gare de Lyon. She was welcomed into the anonymous, hurried mass of commuters, whose eardrums are overwhelmed by the chaotic concert of announcements and information spewing out of loudspeakers, accompanied by the noise of shoes beating the floor in a steady rhythm. In this familiar setting, Christelle acted by instinct, walking as she usually would, head down, back slightly bent, accustomed to the mask of rush hour on exhausted faces with no smiles that kept moving past her. An interminable parade of features, colors, clothes, sizes, thousands of destinies meeting for a fraction of a second, blank stares colliding for an instant and then ignoring each other forever. Every day, Christelle heard the depressing echo of these silences. She kept walking, her pace dictated by the hustle and bustle of the crowd. Dazzled by the overpowering, blinding neon lights, she squinted and then looked up to verify the times. Always on the move, a prisoner of the rapid chaotic swell. Impossible to stop herself. The *clickety clack* of train stations going by at an unheard-of pace on the display panel until it suddenly stopped on a destination, a number or a letter indicating the platform. At the shrill sound of the train horn, a human tide would converge on the same escalator. Christelle participated in this merciless mad rush twice a day. It worked. Everyone just got swallowed up by cars in haphazard gulps, a chaotic ballet of automatons, exhausted from their daily work.

The crowd carried Christelle to the train that was waiting for her. Accustomed to the routine, she was among the first to enter and quickly find a seat. Discreet, never wanting to disturb anyone, she found a seat in the middle of the car, farthest away from the draft. She sat with her back to the direction in which

　　　　　　　Wilfried N'Sondé

the train was traveling. She sank all the weight of her exhausted body onto the seat, ready to savor the ever-so-slight feeling of getting away.

She was surprised when she recognized the melancholic young man she had passed on the Pont d'Austerlitz much earlier.

I was sitting in front of her, terrified, with even more pain and bitterness in my expression. She saw that I was frightened! Christelle carefully scrutinized my tormented face and my pupils, dilated from anxiety, then closed her eyes.

THE DAY ON the bridge, a broken soul, I was not dreaming. Squinting beneath the setting sun, my gaze had simply gotten lost in the river's filth. Horrible images of war and flames were rumbling deep down inside me. At times, I was thinking of Marcelline and the rare honeymoon hours of our childhood, my lips on her shoulder, the tender taste of the first quivers that are never spoken. These treasures with her, I secretly cherished them. Her absence was making my heart bleed, constantly reminding me of what I had become, a pathetic reflection of humanity, inconsequential, a shipwrecked victim of happiness . . . An illegal alien!

An infinite silence in my soul, an abyss, beyond fear and doubt, a sharp pain in the gut, immense uncertainty, worse than a feeling of malaise. Emptiness, absolute despair.

Every day, I kept a low profile in Paris, walking with my head down and staring at my feet to avoid looking in front of me. I had forgotten all about the dream, which risked ending up in bureaucracy, a file with some numbers stamped on it. I was running away, heading nowhere, to avoid being detained, confined behind bars, with wrists and ankles handcuffed, accused of having tried everything, defied every unimaginable danger, flirted with death a thousand times, suffered everyone's contempt, and all I wanted was simply to live! A misdemeanor of hope, a crime of dreams, of better days! The last few months, I had been living a nightmare with no future in sight. From early morning until late afternoon, I spent sleepless nights in insalubrious places, ten or more of us occupying a few square meters. The misery I was carrying around was especially noticeable in my resignation and lack of self-esteem.

I wandered for hours on foot or bicycle in the scorching July heat or during the worst November days. Unnoticed. I saw walls everywhere, even inside me! I had escaped my country in filthy clothes, there where you were dying slowly but surely, anywhere, at any given moment! In Paris, I had become yet another anonymous soul among the worst dregs of society, broken, to be swept away by any means, in an airplane or to a camp, with police vans, police officers with clear consciences, clubs, and despised by everyone. An illegal immigrant.

~

The day I met Christelle, I had spent the afternoon on a public bench. As usual, I was basically staying out of sight to avoid the looks that made me feel like a pariah. I was waiting it out, trying to escape by blending the unbearable images of my past with the gray sky and the concrete, with the cacophony of the deafening metallic sounds of the street. I was fighting a losing battle against the cold, this venomous, loyal daily companion, distilled by this world that never failed to close its doors to me and had nothing to offer me. Sitting on the bench, I would occasionally caress the cold change for the meal of the day, a baguette or a tin of sardines, that I held firmly in my hands, buried in my pants pockets.

That same morning, a former militia comrade had asked me to move out after having put me up for almost a month. His wife refused to keep bumping into me in the apartment during the day. She was afraid I would frighten their children. For her,

I was an animal at bay, today in chains but potentially extremely dangerous. Illegal, I had neither friend nor fellow countryman. I had basically left at the crack of dawn, one foot in front of the other, my expression more somber than ever, absent, alone on the streets of Paris, excluded from happiness, wearing dirty, holey socks.

~

On the bridge, I gathered whatever courage I had left to confront the test of the train station, filled with patrol officers and anti-riot officers, residence permits, criminal investigation operations! I was so anxious, my stomach was knotted up and my jaw was clenched. I waited for darkness to fall so that I could sneak my way into the crowded Gare de Lyon and take a train heading to a shelter for homeless people way out in the suburbs.

Once I entered the huge concourse, my pulse was racing at my temples, literally like a furnace in my head, totally obsessed with the idea of not standing out. The mere sight of the blue of a police officer's uniform immediately set off a terrible panic in me.

My muscles stiffened suddenly when I saw a police roadblock about ten meters in front of me. Plainclothes cops, with cold penetrating gazes, orange armbands that read police, examining the crowd suspiciously, randomly choosing candidates for an ID check.

A rush of adrenaline exploded in my chest. Completely derailed by fear, I found the courage to turn back and head in the opposite direction, away from the crowd, as discreetly as possible. I quickly took off, wandered, and got lost several times. My brain was bubbling over with anxiety, to take off, disappear into the racket of the early evening rush hour. My stomach and throat were seized with cramps. Butt in gear. Do not get caught. My knees wobbled beneath the weight of my fear, and my legs were trembling. Leave this corridor as quickly as possible, toward wherever!

In my distress, I had to hold on to the fight for life with the tenacity of a pesky insect, stand up to the law, be a nuisance, live regardless!

Overcome by a strange intuition, I instinctively got on a train. Convinced that I had become invisible by blending into the crowd, I took a seat next to a window, which would not close properly.

A cold draft gripped me once the train took off, all the more unpleasant because it was mixed in with the scalding heat rising up from beneath the seat. With my hands buried in my pockets, I tried to wedge my body into the soft spot the seat offered. I kept twisting and turning and finally gave in to the discomfort, unable to really relax. I have always been able to live peacefully with suffering.

Busy watching other passengers, on the lookout for a ticket inspector or a police officer, my attention finally zeroed in on the woman sitting in front of me.

CHRISTELLE LET HERSELF get carried by the rhythm of the moving train, in spite of the bumpy ride and the sudden violent shaking caused by trains going in the opposite direction. Her eyes were closed, and her mouth revealed an expression that was difficult to read, a mixture of fatigue and sadness. I looked at her for some time. While staring at her, my breathing gradually slowed and my pulse stabilized. In her simplicity, this woman had touched me. I managed to get a whiff of her scent, a blend of cleanliness and cheap perfume. This universe pleased and comforted me. Seduced, I kept taking her in, her pale face and red hair highlighted with gray strands.

The base of her nostrils was red and irritated, left over from a bad cold. I noticed creases at the corners of her eyes. Christelle's melancholic features moved me, and I was surprised by my reaction. She enveloped me in a whole new feeling, full of sensitivity and kindness.

I looked at her delicate hands, the skin worn from work, but their wrinkles had not made them ugly. Some of her fingers gripped the collar of her coat, and the others held on to her scarf. Melancholy suited her somehow. She was sitting gracefully in her seat, in a way that I had rarely seen in my turbulent life. In her sleepiness, her lips somewhat pursed, she was undoubtedly trying to dismiss, at least for a while, the boredom and lassitude that accompanied her everyday life. She was so amazing to me that I forgot my own fears and began to dream.

~

Christelle inspired words I had never known, inaudible exchanges between couples I saw walking through the city at the end of the day, hand in hand, immersed in a passionate discussion. I envied them especially when they were kissing. Secretly, I admired the women laughing their hearts out, throwing their heads back while in the arms of their beloved. Her lover passes his hand through her hair, they look each other intensely in the eyes, a quick, gentle kiss, she rests her head delicately on his shoulder.

I have always experienced happiness as a spectator, like one who intrudes on its beauty, a poor ignorant bastard. I was never the good friend, invited home to dinner, or the guy you presented to your mother.

~

After several stations, as we sat there alone in front of each other in a one-of-a-kind face-to-face, the silhouettes of two uniformed police officers appeared at the back of the car. Brutally jolted from my dream, I suddenly returned to my skin as the absent one, illegal, the monster who frightens, the villainous beast no one wants to resemble. Consumed by the fear of an uncertain future, I was suddenly overcome by a violent urge to scream out the rage lurking deep within me.

I wanted to plead humbly with arms outstretched to the sky. I repressed my cry; fear suffocated my desire. Resigned, sadness flooded my eyes, and in the end I just lowered them.

When I raised my eyes a few seconds later, Christelle timidly reached out and touched my leg with her fingers and smiled!

SOME TIME AFTER the train's departure from Paris, Christelle was already dozing off. She recalled Sunday afternoons at her parents' home in the suburbs, the family seated at the table for lunch, rays of sunlight and joy. Some sunny images of the past. She took a deep breath.

She had already been working as a nurse's aide at Pitié-Salpêtrière hospital for fifteen years, irregular hours, day shifts, night shifts, weekends. In the end, it had caused her marriage to break up and destroyed her health. She was now living alone in a two-room apartment in the suburbs of southeast Paris, to be as close as possible to her job. The train to Gare de Lyon, then the bus, and a little walk, when the weather was pleasant. She loved her job. In fact, it was all that she knew how to do! Being close to the sick, especially children and the elderly, helping the most unfortunate, whom she graced with her smile. She took great care to groom them gently and diligently. The nurse's aide willingly cleaned and purified broken bodies defiled by diseases.

Although she did not really admit it to herself, the interest some patients showed in the breasts they imagined beneath her uniform was reassuring to her. She missed her twenties and the firm curves she used to have beneath tight, smooth skin. Sitting at the edge of hospital beds, she listened patiently to the wailings and complaints, always the same ones. Christelle took some pleasure from the caresses that would linger at times on her leg. In those moments, she felt beautiful and desirable. When persistent patients would request special favors, she would slowly get up, move her index finger from left to right, gently reproachful, her cheeks flushed a little, and then leave the room, flattered. Her hands in the pockets of her uniform would pull the fabric even closer to her rear end, in the unexpressed hope that an onlooker might linger for a while on her movements.

Life for her was about making others happy! In the rooms and sanitized corridors, Christelle played out the show in which she was convinced she had the leading role, beyond all the tubes, syringes, the shit and death. She was that gentle breeze that comforted. With a quick and supple step, she beamed as she floated into the space of pain that over the years had become the only place where she was expected, recognized, and really existed. Outside the hospital, Christelle was invisible to everyone, until the evening our paths crossed on the train!

When she opened her eyes briefly, she caught me looking at her. I was ashamed, convinced that she found me ugly. Later, I learned that she had detected something mysterious and tender in my face, even if she had told herself not to let anything show and to keep her distance. She burst out laughing when she insisted that I certainly did not seem ugly, more like a big baby, lost, looking for a mother!

After a delay, I finally turned my head away. She found my embarrassment sweet. Truth be told, Christelle had been flattered that I had been looking at her in her sleepy state, she for whom dreams had some time ago been violated through despair and monotony. There was a sparkle in her eyes, lost in the distant glimmer of cities, distorted in a lackluster yellow light by the speed of the train.

The same trip every day. Silence and absence defined the rhythm of her days. Christelle often wore a sad expression with dark circles under her eyes, deprived of tears, which no longer streamed down her face. Bored, she was resigned to a life in which her body was forgotten in the shadow of old flames and dreams, and she was left to celebrate her desires through the solitary pleasures of her hands.

My embarrassment felt like a gentle shiver on her skin, a caress beneath her breasts. She sighed and closed her eyes, but this time with a tender smile. Despite my disgraceful appearance, I had managed to send waves of sweet sensations to her far-too-often-mistreated heart.

~

Like mine, her heart had been broken during her childhood, a nightmare that haunts her and works on her behind her veil of oblivion even to this day. The shadows of her stepfather's gaze and hands on her bare thighs. All the years of feeling defiled. A bitter wound in her stomach, a hideous scar covering the memory of it all. No matter how hard she tried to chase these images away, they would not disappear. And especially the horror of being prey to the voraciousness of his greedy, crazy eyes, like feed, without the slightest help from her mother. Since then, she bore the weight of this burden of distress, this unspeakable ill, embedded in her body. Christelle often experienced herself as dirty.

She had forgotten the desire to love after her first love, the one to whom she had given her body and so much of her soul, had left her for her best friend. Ever since her trust had been broken again, persistent emptiness and doubt haunted her and kept her isolated. The wounds from this betrayal were still bleeding in her chest, obsessive, bright red marks.

Years of marriage, childless, marked by silence, alcohol, and beatings. She eventually realized that they had never really known each other. Fear. Boredom. An exhausting job, an unemployed husband, fewer and fewer caresses. When he finally stopped beating her, some weeks went by, and then he disappeared. Today, she consoles herself with flings that have no possible future.

Her last lover, an attentive, gentle teacher, had proudly named her Venus of the train station. Divinity, grace, and beauty, she melted into happiness and for several weeks could not stop the tears from flowing. One Monday morning, after coffee and the usual see-you-later kiss on the mouth, he also disappeared, leaving neither an address nor a farewell note, instead a wreckage of questions without answers and multiple open fractures in her heart. In the beginning, she could not even make out the difference between day and night. She lost the courage to get up in the morning and forgot even the taste of water. Then she would scream to the point of almost destroying her vocal chords, banging her head against the wall, and scratching the skin of her face and her arms until they bled. Exhausted, empty on the inside, and voiceless. Her doctor prescribed tranquilizers and a lot of rest. The medication wiped her out.

~

Christelle was confined for an entire week in a psychiatric hospital.

~

Sometimes, when she looked in the mirror, she would recall how young and pretty she used to be, a sensational redhead in another life, but that was some years ago now. She had barely had the chance to notice her own body changing, blood flowing from between her legs, her breasts budding and filling out, firm and round, before there was an army of lecherous gazes following her every move. It was difficult to hide her curvaceous figure, which she tried so painfully to live with. Men were always looking at her as though they had suddenly tucked their brains in their pockets. She was convinced that most of them had no clue how to even use their brains.

～

Lost in her memories, she had forgotten about me for a few moments. The blaring alarm of the train brought her back to me. There was one last station before she would have to brave the cold and return to her solitude.

～

She looks at me maternally when she explains how I was holding my head down, my wrists in my pocket, sad; it just broke her heart. Christelle had the impression that I was crying. She looked at my cheeks. It seemed to her there were minuscule tears, pearls of sadness, rivers of bitterness, beneath my eyes, streaming down with little sobs. She instinctively leaned toward me and, in a voice full of tenderness, asked me what was the matter!

THE JAM-PACKED TRAIN that had been filled with an anonymous mass at the time of departure from Paris had gradually
emptied out, leaving us to experience its halting rhythm. The
only view on the other side of the windows was of the well-lit
train stations. They followed each other, each one resembling the
other, peopled with shadows taking hurried steps that came
together and disappeared in the darkness of the late afternoon.
Inside, the artificial white light—the one that lays everything
bare—a narrow aisle separating the blue and red seats, the floor,
a dull and dirty gray, where all our desires and repressed words
wound up.

Two friendly police officers passed by, greeted us with a
simple "Evening," and continued nonchalantly on their way.

⁓

I had escaped the ID check to which I had otherwise resigned myself. I raised my head to see Christelle's smile, full of
kindness. Convinced that, by some miracle, she had just saved
me from a catastrophe, I stared at her as you might at a fairy. She
could read the infinite gratitude in my eyes. Surprised and em-
barrassed by my reaction, Christelle felt a little uncomfortable
in her seat.

Surprised, we found ourselves alone, sitting very close to each other, face-to-face, strangers to each other. Something unsettling took over the carriage space. For a few seconds, we remained speechless. Lost sentences beneath our tongues quieted in our gaze, two solitudes seeking each other out, evading and glancing at each other from the corners of our eyes, behind the barrier of silence.

～

I squelched what little pride I had left and miraculously gathered up my remaining courage to respond to her in a pathetic voice. Possessed suddenly by subtle and tender spirits, I spoke from my heart.

I was hoping to go to a shelter for the homeless, and I got lost along the way! A huge knot suddenly lodged itself in my throat and stifled my voice. I had the hardest time getting out the fact that I really had no place to go to!

Christelle's heart suddenly ignited. She admitted to recognizing the pain from her own life in my eyes. I was going adrift, calling out to her for rescue. A broken man had spontaneously opened up to her. She had never before experienced such sincerity. She invited me to get off with her and have a drink. Together, we would come up with a solution.

My name is Christelle. She held out her hand. Clovis . . . My name is Clovis Nzila!

She had a good laugh, pointing out that only a black person could have such a bizarre first name. It made her happy, gave her the carefree air of a mischievous little girl. For a while, the light glowing on her cheeks chased away the veil of pain that so often covered her.

～

I followed her onto the platform. We left the train station, crossed the street, and went into the first café we saw.

SITTING IN THE back of the café at the train station, Christelle and I avoided looking directly at each other. It was strange for her to find herself with a much younger man who came from so far away. It was my first time being alone with a woman. I had no clue how to behave. I felt kind of stupid. I kept stealing a glance here and there, looking at the decor of wooden furniture and the black-and-white pictures. Christelle was even more beautiful.

She regretted not having ordered an alcoholic drink. Occasionally, she would have one, then she would start crying for no apparent reason, to erase unpleasant memories and sink into a deep and dreamless sleep before a difficult awakening. Always a little too much to drink, to forget the days of fear, of the time spent in the psychiatric hospital and the weeks convalescing in the countryside, an interminable winter of treatments undertaken in complete calm. To think, no more long months to spend trying painfully to put her life back together. Years had gone by, and yet she still felt weak and fearful. She took her time, looking carefully at me. Christelle placed her lips delicately on the steaming cup of hot chocolate. Strangely, I felt that my presence calmed her. Her face lit up with a huge smile before she spoke to me in a clear voice.

Christelle chatted about unimportant matters, just to break the ice, and then finally asked me some specific questions.

In my confusion, Christelle kept getting closer to me, even as I was falling apart right in front of her. Sincerely sorry, without having a clear idea of what to say, she mumbled some words of consolation and then suggested that she could put me up for the night; it was already so late, and as for the rest, we would figure it out in the morning.

She talked to me about a stew she had prepared that same morning.

I was so grateful to her for having chosen to trust me right away.

"I don't live too far away; let's hurry. It's pretty cold out this evening!"

I could hardly believe my luck. I was so used to living on high alert. Bad luck had pretty much governed my life up until this point. For so long, my heart pulsated only with rage and the will to survive at all costs. Following a perfect stranger at nightfall in a country that I knew practically nothing about was somehow so ordinary to me. Anything was worth trying to escape the police. After all, nothing could possibly compare to years of civil war. I had rubbed shoulders with death so many times that it felt like freedom to me. The militia had broken me down and toughened me up; I had become practically indestructible!

No one had ever helped me, with the exception of my sister. I would have much preferred to have my outstretched hands chopped off by a machete than accept help from anyone.

Feeling anxious and awkward, I was sweating like a pig even though it was so cold. Memories of myself as a snotty-nosed unloved kid came back to me, the bullying, slanders, and injustices. And here I was once again at the mercy of a woman. I was afraid. My pulse was racing at such a crazy pace that it was impossible to slow it down. My knees were shaking. There was a huge knot in my throat. My mouth was dry.

⁓

As for Christelle, she swore not to repeat the same mistakes. At the first insult, the slightest sign of disrespect, she would throw me out without even bothering to understand or trying to explain.

I love it when she tries to be strict, wearing her serious face. She looks at me with a not-so-convincing pout that wants to be threatening. I pretend to listen to her religiously and have to stop myself from bursting out into a fit of laughter so as not to upset her.

⁓

Things happened so quickly. We barely knew each other. It was really just about her helping me out and me thanking her, but within the first hours, a strong bond formed between us, and we found ourselves at the epicenter of a magical vortex of curiosity, yearnings, and desires.

⁓

Concentrating, Christelle chose the words to use and the expressions to avoid. For fear of being herself and disappointing, she hid behind a kind of artifice and pretense. She lived distanced from her real self, obsessed by the idea she might appear clumsy or vulgar. Did not want to be a flop at first impressions. She was of an age at which she could finally be considered a lady.

⁓

When speaking of her joy and sadness, Christelle had only one way of addressing them, with few words. She had accumulated expressions laboriously over the course of her sad, uneducated existence. Those of the streets disgusted her, the brouhaha from the television annoyed her, and as for the rest, she did not understand a thing! It all came out of her in a big jumble. She repeated banalities of no interest whatsoever. Once she had finished, she would roll her eyes inquiringly, blush, and then lower them.

Seconds later, she was out of her jail, dreaming of becoming a woman who was sure of her direction, with an athletic and elegant silhouette, chest high and shoulders pulled back. Looking straight ahead, sure of her qualities, almost haughty, keeping vulgarity and baseness at arm's length. Hair down, styled to perfection like the great beauties of cinema. Christelle pictured herself able to appeal to the world and arouse a sense of wonder. She would have loved to be that girl for whom the richest, most handsome men suffer, those who never make dirty love. The ones who take you to a dance and would give anything, no matter what, just to have the pleasure of kissing your hand.

Christelle had opened her heart too often, given her body over for the price of a kiss, for a little bit of attention, for three or four cheap compliments, a pale imitation of real love. Men took her roughly and quickly, in a confusion of sweat, the smell of beer and cold tobacco. All crowned with a bestial grunt, a vague sort of baby-that-was-so good-I-love-you kiss on the lips.

The man then turns away and departs into his world of snoring. Unsatisfied, a dreamer, she remains cold.

Christelle preferred not to say anything so that she could avoid hearing these types of sentences, which, once out of her mouth, made her realize they should never have been said and were now impossible to take back. All these trivial sounds jostling clumsily against one another the moment they rolled off her tongue.

⁓

Side by side, our faces were being whipped by the cruel easterly winds in the poorly lit alleyway. Gradually, our steps became synchronized.

Christelle just wanted me to be kind to her. She blushes when she tells me that she had already started to think about making herself pretty on the way home, tackling her hair, which had become rust-colored and silvery after vain attempts to color it, to try to silence the disturbing message that more and more gray hairs were on the way. She would meticulously wax her underarms, her legs, and her mons pubis and finally highlight the gray tones that adorned her thin red mane. She had come to realize that it was absurd to try to wage a war against time and imagine that grace, charm, and beauty were not the privileges of youth. The meandering paths traced out on the skin of her hips and her stomach, tell the story of years gone by. Whoever had the know-how to advance with the necessary curiosity, precision, and especially the respect due to the sacred would be lucky enough to have access to her. Thanks to the ruthless nature of time, which keeps moving forward, suffering had taught her to love her ever-changing body and curves.

I was so proud that she had chosen me. We were slipping into the craziness of love.

❧

Christelle and I, we had connected. She had brought me into her universe. Her words gave me hope and enveloped me in an aura of light in my solitary night.

ONCE WE ARRIVED at her apartment, frequently occupied by silence, Christelle was happy to have someone coming in with her. She invited me in and told me to make myself at home!

For a place to sleep, she could offer me only the old sofa bed. It squeaked a little if you moved on it, but I should be OK for one night.

To mask her nervousness, she busied herself around the apartment and went on about nothing. Her daily routine found its place in my answers and the sounds and scents of the life we were sharing, almost naturally. Did I mind excusing her for a minute? She had to go warm up the dinner, she would not be too long!

Seated quietly at one end of the sofa, my hands tucked between my thighs, I thanked Christelle for her hospitality. At the same time, my intimidated eyes circled around this new, modest, and tidy world. Some family photos—parents laughing, a little boy pouting, and an adolescent girl with a melancholic expression. A flowerpot, a vague feeling of cleanliness, no expression of fantasy, Christelle's universe.

The anxiety of the unknown coupled with the lure of discovering something new gave me a tingling sensation in my stomach and a stiffness in my gestures, all the clumsier because I did not know how to make myself useful. Once the table was set, I sat in front of her. I tasted for the first time what was called "dinner at home."

&

Two strangers, sitting face-to-face, timidly exchanging trivialities, giving each other meaningful glances. Furtive looks and forced smiles designed to encourage trust between us. A modest meal with simple gestures and everyday words took on the allure of a real feast. Short sentences, sometimes inaudible, awkward, and unclear. Such balm for two souls abandoned by life. The warmth of another person giving birth to hope. No longer feeling alone in the world, at least not in this moment.

After dinner, Christelle disappeared to take a shower. When she came out of the bathroom, she found me already sleeping soundly, fully dressed, on the sofa, undone by fatigue and relieved by the feeling that I could finally just let myself go and relax.

&

Before completely closing my eyes, I found the softness of my sister's arm and the perfume of her skin on the tip of my tongue. Marcelline, my beloved twin, my beacon in a fog of distress. This forbidden love, following the time shared in the liquid pocket in the darkness of the maternal womb, when the world consisted of only her and me.

&

While I slept, Christelle looked at me with tenderness and a hint of pity.

&

She tucked me in maternally before heading to her room. She tiptoed to avoid making even the smallest sound and then gently closed the door. Christelle fell asleep, snuggled up deep in her bed. I secretly hoped she would dream about me.

Help, help! Hours passed before my screams ripped into the quiet of the night. I woke up in a panic, caught in a nightmare.

Suddenly, I recovered, but I could not control the howling coming from my throat. My heart was beating so fast I wished I could rip it out with my fingers. I would have done just about anything to escape this torture. Huge drops of sweat accumulated on my forehead. I was afraid to wake up Christelle. I could not control myself. I was imprisoned within myself and my own suffering. My clothes stuck to my skin.

It had been hard leaving my country behind, the land of my ancestors, my childhood; the drama of my very existence was etched between my skin and my soul, determined not to let go of me. I was dragging my disaster along with me like a ball and chain. Impossible for me to turn my back on the past and make that big break and advance toward new possibilities, the hope for a life of stars, happiness.

Without hesitating, Christelle came running to me as she was in the habit of doing with her patients.

Calm down, nothing happened, it was just a bad dream. She is here now! Christelle was serene. She was not frightened at all. She kept massaging my head and my face and whispering soothing words. I was ashamed and kept apologizing profusely. It felt good, her full bosom, the magic of her curves. Without even realizing it, Christelle was taming a ferocious beast. She gathered me into her strong arms, curled me into her supple body, a fully realized femininity.

"Tell me about your dream if you want to; you'll feel better. Trust me, I won't hurt you!"

Christelle had closed her eyes and whispered her words.

I thought about the nightmare, fought hard to gather my memories. What could I do about yesterday, with my regrets, with the marks branded with red-hot iron, with the indelible fault? My past mistakes were eating me up and weighing heavily on me.

It all began in the heartland, following the great counsel of Nzambi A Mpoungou, the creator of all that we can and cannot see. On the dawn of the first day, the World slowly glided from between her legs to meet up with light. From her entrails, she created the jungle, animals, stones, rivers, majestic cliffs, creeks, cascades, and mountains. When the storm came, she had cried frozen poles, glacier tongues, powerful oceans, interior seas, immense lakes to hide her most precious fish and even the little streams that run right beneath the eyelids of men when the noose of sadness tightens firmly around their hearts.

~

Profoundly asleep, the goddess dreamed she had covered the earth with vibrant colors. She shook a moment in her sleep and blew winds and storms under all skies.

~

She is the Mother of the World, who guides those hands that explore the whole body to soothe, seduce, and electrify. Love, love! From the wombs of women, children were born, the fruit of a cry of pain. She gave them the smile to lighten the days and an irresistible magical charm in their eyes to comfort and illuminate their darkest nights. In rare moments of divine fatigue, she let anger and death escape, ax and wound. Everywhere, there was resistance and loss. Capricious, impatient, she huffed and puffed and growled violence and hate that went about parading proudly everywhere, more tenacious than eternal snow, fiercer and more cunning than birds of prey, but far less majestic.

Awoken one morning by the most amazing inspiration, illuminated, Nzambi A Mpoungou covered the whole earth with a virtually imperceptible music, of hearts beating, of the sound of skin in contact with the World. She placed a magical thread that supports and heals to accompany men and women across time in their dreams, gestures, and ideas. The pact that connects the living and the dead: the kiss of the spirits!

The invisible flow that gives greatness and meaning to matter. The goddess created the spirits by gathering into her hands the beauty of those hearts that have gone on before. She blessed them and granted them the power of never-ending love and let them enter into the world of the living. Full of wisdom, they accompanied and consoled.

Nonchalantly, and with a tender gesture, she scattered multitudes of spirits of great wisdom among countless mammals. In an elegant and gentle surge, they lavished intoxicating colors and magical perfumes, and we heard them intone in chorus a sweet song, love, love! Pleased to see her most precious caprices so alive, Nzambi A Mpoungou opened the discussion.

～

For the big reunion, she summoned the earth, the wind, the great oceans, His Eminence, life, animal power, the strength of plant life, and noble minerals. Death would arrive later, sheepish and frazzled, unable to hide its embarrassment. Forever gentle and carefree, the spirits spun around cheerfully every which way, caressing and comforting wherever they went. Love, love, they hummed, with that peaceful smile from their creator.

Death responded in a worrisome, deep voice. Challenged by the melody, it realized that fatigue from slavery, colonization, wars and massacres for independence, coups d'état, famines, waste, and civil wars, all this work on earth had culminated in exhaustion! And so, rather than consulting with the great counsel, death ignored the enthusiastic murmurs of the spirits and, with cowardice and in the greatest secrecy, asked its sisters, misery and horror, to help finish the job. Afraid of being overwhelmed and subsequently disappointing, misery and horror called on their cousin barbarity to come to the rescue and finish the dirty work. Death.

Love, love!

In a strangled voice, sobbing in rage and shame, you could hear death apologizing to life, an occurrence unique since the beginning of time. Never, not even for a moment, had it ever imagined that catastrophe could take on such magnitude!

Regretful, Nzambi A Mpoungou witnessed the earth become panic-stricken, trying in vain to breathe life into the millions of humans recently buried in its bosom.

Unfortunately, you cannot play around with barbarity! How do you gather up eyes that have been ripped out, hands that have been severed and scattered about, arms, legs? Frustrated, the earth began to tremble, randomly, anywhere and everywhere, expanding the scale of the disasters.

From above, you could hear the ancestors of the world, the lords of the bush and the forests, and men, prostrated before their errors. Disregarding the ravages of death, humans were designated singularly responsible for the disorder and carnage, for unleashing their contempt and polluting the earth with their murderous breath. A lowly, narrow-minded person had foiled the efforts of worldwide medicine. People were dying in Paris, New York, Brazzaville, as far off as Beijing.

This anger, like the worst of calamities, got into the heads of children. With brains blinded by a destructive craziness, they massacred their fathers with machetes and then raped their mothers and sisters. "Love, love," the spirits repeated, panic-stricken. Already, disaster and chaos hovered like absolute masters of an impasse, and no one knew how to go about fixing things. The spirits cried. Had they already fallen silent? Had they distanced themselves, become forever voiceless because of envy, hate, and machine guns?

~

Have mercy, my son, love; the whole world was created from one and the same vulva! That's the truth. Women, men, animals, stones, the world is born every day. We live off its breasts. Spare me, my son, we're all brothers!

I can still remember the old man, at my mercy. He had told me that story to save his skin . . .

Crazed with anger, I found his story suspect. My superior in the militia, Admiral Rambo, shut him up with a blow to the mouth from the butt of his gun. Seconds later, emotionless, he plunged a metallic pointed object straight into the old man's eye, right through to his brain. I never knew that such a puny body could contain that much blood!

~

Since that time, I have tried to regain the innocence of the newborn, registered under the name of Clovis Nzila, in the service of the Lingolo commune, but that memory of my comrade's cruelty has never ceased to haunt me.

~

Stunned, shocked, something froze violently in Christelle's stomach. She found herself facing a cataclysm of sobbing, violence, and screaming. Her heart was racing a mile a minute from shock and horror. All the same, she was tender toward me, crying uncontrollably in her arms, my warm body completely abandoned next to hers.

~

The first time I had that bad dream, I woke up in a sweat, startled, screaming for help, trapped among other refugees, fugitives, and dying people. My whole body trembled. The mere reflection of that old man's expression speaks to me and reproaches me. He is still looking at me, always, always . . .

Since birth, I have been easily carried away with hate and anger. I was always crying and sneering at my life.

Surrounded by strangers, in a minivan, I crossed cities, deserts, forests, dangerous and hostile countries, cold penetrating my skin and my chest filled with fear. I was heading toward the unknown on the path that should have led me to paradise. I was running away with despair at my heels. On that night, the animal I had always been shuddered with the fear of those deprived of their own destiny.

Always calm, Christelle listened to me with the beauty you grant to a child's confessions.

~

Timidly, I evoked the madness of the admiral and my other comrades and the blood. We reigned over the lives of others and determined their fates. Brutal deaths for my friends, who were among the most loyal, Lord-of-Death and One-Eye-Two-Words. I recognized the head of one of them on a pickax brandished by those more ferocious than us. The other one was finished off with kicks from the admiral's boots during a night of heavy drinking and rage.

~

Locked away in shame, I slowly reclaimed control of my life amid the sobbing. I dared to ask for forgiveness. Christelle took my hands in hers and covered them with tears . . .

A FEW HOURS before, Christelle's only thought had been about some well-deserved rest. Sore from so much work, she had hoped to soak her body in a hot bath of rich foam and soothing perfumes. Then she would slide under the clean, comfy sheets of her huge bed and try to fall asleep right away, flee far away from herself, as quickly as possible!

In the middle of the night, my host found herself consoling a total stranger, a volcano of distress. In her tender arms, I was battling it out with myself, absolutely destitute. Agitated, I collapsed on the floor, moving every which way. She used all her strength to pull me up between her legs and calm me down, somewhat surprised all the same by my body's contact with her exposed private parts.

In an intense whirlpool of tears, horrific, unforgivable, inconceivable cruelty came to be confessed in her living room. The ugliness of this world was staying in her home, his head nestled on her belly, seeking absolution.

Speak, you'll feel better! Something greater than her own will urged Christelle to take in my humanity, shattered to pieces, instead of getting rid of me, this person coming from someplace she barely noticed on the television while doing her nails. She had never really understood anything about these black people on television warring with each other every day, not to mention the scrawny-looking children with their Biafra bellies, broadcast at dinnertime.

Sentimental by nature, Christelle was always sensitive to those who cried out and asked for help. Confused, her mother never really understood and would say that her daughter was born with her heart on her sleeve, her face illuminated like an angel's. It never even crossed her mind to throw out a war veteran in dire straits. She was not going to let me wander off into the night, riddled with guilt and grief, she said compassionately, be kind to me always!

Perhaps I gave her the chance to rise above the abandonment and despair in which she had buried herself for some time, alone, with no one by her side. Her arms opened up to me who did not deserve it. Her determined and gracious heart was ready to take off together toward new heights!

She was sure that I was different in every way from all the men she had known before because I was not telling her beautiful lies and I was not ready to immediately climb onto her curvaceous body and let my pleasure explode all over her. My words had stirred hidden recesses within her. She could feel that I was simple and sincere, to be honest, a little strange, but not pretentious or affected!

Someone was finding refuge and peace in the depths of her body, simply because it was her and she was there!

Her presence soothed me. I let myself be soothed by the maternal sounds of her voice. She hummed: I'd like to take you to a magical country where mauve flower petals drink up the sun, sweeter than kisses.

An echo in the silence. A barely discernible murmur.

Christelle embraced me, a slow fusion of solitudes in the movement of our awkward bodies, cautious dreams, quivering gestures of two people thirsty for intense emotions and affection.

My physical appearance, my awkward features, my unsightly looks, Christelle had already buried them in the desert of superficiality, tucked them away, folded them up, and forgotten them along with her age and wrinkles. I implored her to help me live again. I was so alone!

I am afraid to fall asleep. My nights are sleepless. I keep seeing the silhouette of Admiral Rambo, beating on the deafening drums of desolation, so intensely that I scream for my life, without being able to hear my own voice. I am obsessed with all of this, and it is making me crazy!

Christelle wanted me to talk a little about myself! She felt strong and ready to hear everything from the beginning. She would weave wings around my fears so my wounds would disappear, take off, far away, free me from the sinister character that continues to frighten me.

If a country of forgiveness could exist, she was going to use our hands to build it, use this new strength together.

"I will relieve you of the horrors so that you can find peace!"

Cradled in her tenderness, my memory took a cautious leap forward and then ran up painfully against shame and remorse. It then wandered off into the hiding places of oblivion. What had really happened? Christelle waited calmly and attentively. Little by little, memory filled with courage and zoomed in on the sad days buried deep within my past.

HER NAME WILL be Marcelline! My life began with these words. These were, it is said, the last words that our mother, Rose Nzila, spoke, her hands resting on the little girl she had just brought into the world after a long day of unbearable suffering. Exhausted, drained of a huge amount of blood, relieved, she joined the universe of those who had gone on ahead of her. Before the women who had been helping her could start to cry, they realized that something was moving inside her belly.

It had to be a really bad miracle to give birth to a twin brother. I was a hideous, poorly developed baby. They called me "Clovis," the name of my alleged father. He had denied being responsible for the pregnancy of his domestic help of fifteen years. Our mother had been beaten black and blue by both the mistress of the house and her occasional lover before being sent back to her village in the countryside without a dime.

The tragedy of our mother, whom we never knew, finally came to an end. Her only consolation was the respect she earned, however posthumously, for being the mother of twins.

Such children are venerated because they possess the ability to decipher the invisible world. The woman who gives birth to them also acquires a special status. Yet everyone in the village agreed that this birth was a bad omen. It crossed their minds to bury the children alive and put an end to it all. But the girl, my sister, was so cute that the idea of causing her harm was already heartbreaking. As for me, the boy, I apparently inspired only disgust and fear. No one wanted my evil spirit to haunt the village if by misfortune they did away with me.

Swearing Vulva, penis! as was her habit, our grandmother Louise decided to adopt us. Not only had she in no way benefited from her daughter's situation living with one of the big fish in the capital, but now she was left alone to educate her offspring because Mademoiselle could not keep her legs closed and had gotten herself pregnant. Vulva penis! She loved to shock. With her hard heart, the old lady did not seem in the least affected by the loss of her daughter. In fact, she had refused to be present for the deliveries. That she was able to cherish little Marcelline, fair-skinned and as beautiful as the day, was OK, but to throw in the boy, this runt, ugly and as black as night, it was just too much to bear in a life already full of so much hardship. Had she not suffered enough? She spat violently, stomped her foot, and lit a cigarette.

⁓

Terrorized by the whip of the colonial army, her youth had been nothing but daily trembling and fear. She had experienced World War II, the young men who had been forced to work to death on huge rubber tree trunks. The love of her life had returned to her in the form of a skeletal shadow, his body broken from forced labor. He had been drafted by soldiers, themselves no more than twenty years old, to slave away in the jungle extracting rubber sap that was used to make tires for jeeps and trucks that white heroes, chewing gum and cigars in their mouths, would use to go and bring down Nazi divisions even crueler than they were!

To extract rubber from the equatorial forest, soldiers would kidnap the sturdiest men at night and force them to work by keeping their wives and children hostage. Millions of slaves died, a real carnage, to ensure that the war in Europe was won at all costs!

Following France's liberation, military vehicles parked in the village square, off-loaded a dozen survivors, emaciated specters with bent backs. Her Antoine was returned to her, broken, dying, confused in his speech . . .

They had kissed with tears pouring down. She had sworn and cursed the vulvas and penises of all those who had given birth to such torturers. Those who were fully aware of their status as victors did not have the least thought or pity for the thousands of anonymous victims of their victory. In vain, on her knees, she had invoked the severity of the spirits of justice to spew out onto the pavement under the military parades the blood and bones of all those who had been forgotten. To increase her chance of having her wish granted, she had prayed at length to the mother of the Lord of Nazareth. Convinced that she was a good Christian, she never thought that mixing ancestral worship with worship of Christ was a sin. It is written in the Bible, which she used as she did any other talisman, placing it on the ground in her hut among the other meager objects she had that reminded her of her mother and other family members who had been deceased for quite some time. Since she had never gone to school, Louise had never read one single word of the Bible. Catholicism was the one good that Europeans had brought into her life, even if she was convinced that Jesus, given that he was so good, could not possibly have been white. Joseph and Mary had to have been black in a white country, obliged to give birth to their child in a stable because of the color of their skin.

～

Louise had not had an easy time recognizing her beloved because he had changed so much. He had lost so much weight, his face was emaciated, his ribs were sticking out, and his eyes

　Wilfried N'Sondé

were expressionless. His breathing was labored and weak, with breaths coming between his one or two barely audible expressions of regret. She welcomed him onto the sleeping mat in the back of her hut, to experience a final moment of the love of which they had been robbed.

The sky modestly masked its stars to offer them a night of thick inky black, the sadness of a moan. The wind echoed among the leaves of the big trees, and in the village there was silence. The grave silence of a funeral oration. Louise's tears blended with those of Antoine, a reluctantly delicate kiss on the surface of the lips. He was so fragile that she could easily take him into her arms, console him, and lay him on her naked body. They made love gently. Bony, timid, and tense caresses. Louise felt Antoine's life beating feebly in his stomach. Happy for a moment, she gazed upon the comets in his eyes at the height of pleasure. Antoine passed on in the moment of the final embrace that led to Rose's conception. This first name was chosen so that he would have the same bouquet of flowers in the great beyond with which generals were honored on other continents.

⁓

Since that time, Louise was never known for her kindness. She had systematically abandoned her other children, too soon for some, a bit too late for others. The suffering, the bullying, the injustices had forever ruined her mind. Louise no longer had the least bit of sympathy for humans. Frustrated, she yellowed her index and middle fingers from tobacco in the most revolting way. She must have been the first woman on the continent to smoke in public. No one dared make the least remark about it; they preferred to speak ill quietly among themselves. As for her age, it was indefinable. Behind her back, gossipers claimed that she had been the illegitimate mistress of a famous explorer whose great merit was to have discovered an unknown country where millions of humans had been living for thousands of years. Villagers believed that in the white man's history, glory was distributed at bargain basement prices!

Benevolence was painful for her; vengeance and anger were a source of jubilation. The attention she gave to children came in the form of insults and sound thrashings. Her whole life, this old woman would offer threats when a simple smile or a "thank you" would have been appropriate. Kindness and simplicity got stuck between her lips and were immediately transformed into swearing of the basest kind. She especially hated women for the way they submitted to men, black people in general for their fatalistic attitude before the oppressive whites whom she hated for their inhumanity. Louise struggled, was held captive to an idea of the world that had no resonance or place in her life.

All the years of harboring resentment and suffering had given her a hard face that was closed off and which isolated her a little more every day. She had forgotten the number of marriages she had celebrated after Antoine's death.

To punish her last husband for his infidelity, she castrated him, intoxicating him with magical substances that progressively atrophied his genitals until they finally disappeared. Nganga Jean, a mystery man residing in a remote region, had concocted the especially potent beverage with meticulous cruelty. In fact, only he could bear the company of the old woman. Louise was the only one to call on his services as a healer ever since the women who used to consult with him for fertility issues had given birth to children with eyes as red and bulging as his.

Battling with her chronic misanthropy, Louise brought the newborns to her home, yelling and spitting. She had heard that whites feed their children cow's milk. Hell, now, whatever was good for them was certainly going to be good enough for her bastard grandchildren. Vulva penis!

Moved, Christelle listened carefully to my story. She interrupted at one point.

"I'm so different from you, you know!"

She recalled the weekends in their little suburban home, her mother preparing lunch, her father puttering about doing odd jobs in the garage with her brother, and her, dreaming in her room. Stretched out alone in her bed.

Christelle was surrounded by pink and boredom, her ballet shoes nailed to the wall. She was especially preoccupied with herself. The world was hostile and foreign to her. It did not interest her. She wanted to be pretty and desirable, and yet, for everyone else, Christelle was transparent and invisible. Everybody looked right through her as though she was not there.

Postcards in pastel colors hung on the wall, blurry images of women in summer dresses at the beach. Christelle fed off her frustrations, preoccupied with her moods and feelings. Passive, she waited and complained often, inconsolable. Enclosed in a world of comfort but with not much flair, she settled into reassuring conformity at the expense of her passions and hid herself in the hope of being seen.

"Look at me, I'm hidden!"

～

When I spoke about myself, she was somewhat ashamed. She had the strange and unpleasant feeling that she had lived a carefree life while I had suffered. Happy all the same to learn from me that another world, so close and familiar, did exist.

～

She would have loved to have gotten over herself, out of this prison, to love and share.

Her childhood, a pile of multicolored gifts sitting at the foot of the Christmas tree in December, grandma's chocolate cake for her birthday, always the same, and on it the candles to mark the passing of time. Her stepfather's voice was torture to her ears, not to mention his hypocritical smiles. She and he were forever bound by a horrible secret. And her father, the real one, unknown, she imagined a handsome, strong, magnificent man. He never came back.

During summertime, the sound of the waves of the Atlantic Ocean on the beach in the Basque country lulled her into nostalgia. Every year, the same location at the camping site where her parents had met for the first time. The walk to primary school, her little hand in her mother's, no tenderness or closeness between them.

Her skirts, too short for the boys sitting in front of the entrance to junior high. Her bare legs allowed her to finally break free from anonymity. She existed only to soon disappear again into the fire of their moist eyes. Television every day to get away from herself, have some fun, get some thrills but from a good distance. Absent, imprisoned in a colorless world, passionless, stuck in moderation and trivial worries. Monotonous, routine humming of dull days, holding on to nothing, and hoping for nothing. A fragrant free life punctuated by the challenge of paying bills at the end of the month.

Her mother's cancer and her failed affair with the young guy, a hospital clown, who would later tell her she was far too old for him. Once she had healed, she had offered her body to him, and this intense desire had risen up from within her belly when his lips had collided with hers. An unlikely feeling, a call for help to take off and head to where living means tasting each other with your whole mouth, always walking a tightrope, on the lookout for new forms of craziness.

The one moment of craziness in her life had thrown her husband into a labyrinth of drinking, too cowardly and exhausted to leave it all behind or start over again. Shocked, incapable of taking the time to understand anything at all about the woman who lived right by his side, he preferred to rub his sadness up against the skin of women who were total strangers, jumping into bed with whomever, his heart completely soaked in alcohol. Steal a couple of minutes to dream with the help of some good ole cheap wine.

Weariness and cowardice took over, and they ended up holding on to and consoling each other, paralyzed by the fear of having to stumble separately into the harrowing abyss of uncertainty.

～

Christelle kept going as best she could and hurt herself frequently, abandoned, her body like deadweight, forsaken and helpless. Constantly irritated and dragging her woes along until she succeeded in hating herself.

MARCELLINE AND I grew up in the harshness of rural life below the equator. Up at the crack of dawn, working the fields, gathering wood for the fire, going to fetch water down by the river, endlessly scraping the arid land, backs bent, arms heavy from fatigue, walking for miles under the scorching sun, barefoot, up to our knees in mud after consecutive days of rain, poor harvests, hungry, nights so black you could literally cut them with a knife, recurrent silence, our grandmother spewing out orders in a bad mood, her rage, insults at the tip of her tongue, a firm hand, always ready to hit me and no one to intervene on my behalf. Every day, I heard:

"You're nothing but a bastard. What kind of demon could have impregnated my child to cause her to spawn a monster like you? Look at your sister, as beautiful as the sun, fresh, radiant, a ripe fruit . . . Vulva, penis! You're a real good-for-nothing!"

She did not hit me. No, she bathed me in beatings. They said her beatings were sure to dry out my skin because the palms of her hands were as callous as a lumberjack's!

There was apparently nothing likable about me. They teased me about my skin because it was especially dark, my hideous face, and my body, a real assault on the eyes.

Raised with verbal abuse, contempt and violence, I became devious and cunning. Marcelline meanwhile was lighthearted, beautiful, the pride of the village. The only one to feel sorry for me, to love me. She often cried for me and tried to do my chores for me. On the paths around the village, we were often side by side, ugliness and grace, collapsing under the weight of excessively bulky loads. Me, evil eye, I would contort my body with each step I took, while Marcelline, elegant and gracious and with an un-waveringly good mood, would maintain her stride, sure of her footing, to everyone's delight. Her voice was music, a hymn to life for me, my one and only divinity.

When we were alone, my eyes would burst with joy. I did not speak much; besides, no one listened to me. I existed only in the eyes of my sister. We loved getting off the dirt roads to-gether, setting the loads aside and running into the savanna hand in hand, until we were out of breath. We created a secret world in which there were few words and endless laughter. We would lie there breathless. Even on the ground, we did not let go of each other's hands, panting, carefree, and happy. When our eyes met, they were the eyes of children shining brightly. We would close them to forget the daily routine and create a myriad images of happiness. Precious seconds of life in which to rein-vigorate our spirits and explore the intensity of our shared time in the womb.

The other childhood pleasure we shared, the moment we cherished above all else, occurred at night. In the hut where we lived with our grandmother, we each had our space. However, once her powerful snoring, which I had learned to read and deci-pher, filled the room, I would move closer to Marcelline without making a sound, hold her gently in my arms, and place the tip of my tongue on the velvet softness of her shoulder.

Immobile, Marcelline always pretended to be asleep for some time. She was jubilant. Silently, we re-created the harmony, the shared plenitude of times gone by, when we had been together in our mother's belly. Absorbed in this gentle, fluid universe, each night we fused, filled with a sensation of liquid levitation, of absolute well-being. We continued this rite for many years. We simply had to make sure that we had separated and I had returned to my sleeping spot before our grandmother awoke. Then I would spend the day like a sleepwalker, waiting for the sun to go down.

～

Our happiness was surreptitious. It had taken so much time to rediscover this particular bond we shared, and at any given moment it could come to an end. A few seconds of hesitation, a mistake, and that would be the end of it!

Inevitably, that fatal morning arrived. That cursed day, among so many others. I wanted to enjoy just one final minute of Marcelline's skin. Just one more time, just a little bit more, savor just a couple of seconds. That turned out to be in effect the last time, the prelude to an avalanche of abuse, blows, punches, and kicks. Enraged, the old lady regained her youthful vigor and with a firm stick in hand beat the crap out of me. A flood of anger, the urge to break everything in sight, so that the object of her hatred would become dust, no longer exist. A gaze infused with blood, teeth clenched! She surely would have killed me. Marcelline had to intervene. She suffered so much because of her love for me that she literally passed out. To save her, my grandmother spared me.

They thought she was dead. She was shaking. An unexplainable fever consumed her. She was delirious and kept speaking in an ancient tongue no one understood. Consumed by grief and fear, I ran off into the bush and built myself a makeshift shelter where I could spend the night.

⁓

In the village, the consternation had no limits.

He must have poisoned her, cast a spell on her by having "the sex" with her! The dog, the runt. He was the one who finished Rose off, and now Marcelline, my one and only happiness on this earth. Vulva penis!

Grandmother Louise shouted her rage.

Marcelline's condition between life and death persisted and became worse. They brought in the healer from the neighboring village.

He invoked Nzambi A Mpoungou and numerous redemptive spirits, danced for two whole nights, and concocted some dubious beverages. At several points, he fell into spectacular trances and rolled around in the dust. Naked, he urinated into the fire, confused evil spirits in several huts, denounced an adulterous couple, and predicted a period of disasters for the village.

Hidden at the top of a tree, I watched these scenes in fear and lowered my head in prayer to the spirits and devils to have mercy on her. Bring my sister back to life, I humbly begged.

By the morning of the third day, Marcelline had lost a lot of weight. Her connection to the world of the living had diminished to a shadow of herself with a slight, irregular dilation of her nostrils.

Worn out, the healer was angry that he had not been able to break through the silence of the spirits and penetrate the mystery that was hanging over this girl. Even on her way to the great beyond, she never lost the ability to enchant in a way that appeased whoever encountered her. He pronounced these words:

⁓

"If you want to keep this life, give up another one in exchange! Find a child of the same age, preferably one who's a good-for-nothing, ugly, and dark-skinned!"

❧

The frustrated population did not hesitate for long. Louise, desperate and more vicious than ever, bellowed out the name Clovis, like a death howl to the moon. Track him down like a beast at bay!

❧

They beat the drums, and the hunt began. I took off. Fear immunized me against pain, the branches beat my face, the stones and tree stumps opened the soles of my feet, but nothing could stop me. They would not catch me! Driven by a new superhuman power, I ran off, ignoring all the dangers. No more blows, abuse. Keep going farther and farther away. With death at my heels, I had only to leave this world behind and along with it all the blows . . . I left Marcelline; her absence, torture, irradiated me like a fever.

❧

I carried with me the indelible feel of my tongue on her skin.

CHRISTELLE CRIED FOR some time. During a period of her life when she was just plain old bored, I had suffered so much!

She held me tightly, wanting to protect me from all past misfortunes. If it had been possible for Christelle to plunge into that faraway village, she would have metamorphosed into Marcelline or the goddess of the Earth and found the strength to brush it all away with one full sweep of her hand and accompany me onto a luminous path, a radiant future. She felt my body burning up, stuck to her skin, and smelled a strong, disconcerting odor that men tend to give off, which had unsettled her since her adolescence.

Christelle, that night with you is worth more than my life!

I had touched her and begun to awaken rhythmic throbs in moist skin and a desire to do crazy things.

Christelle was happy taking in the moment. She held me between her arms and legs and ran her hand over my back with discreet and supple movements, body-to-body contact that was chaste and tender.

Because of the sudden, unique way in which Christelle and I had met, we were able to deliver our souls to each other, holding nothing back, and freely draw close to each other.

Hours later, just before dawn, my eyes opened onto this unknown woman, close to me, her deep sensuality, the soothing maturity of her curves, a peaceful discernment. Her belly, a sanctuary for my face and my imagination, a haven for rest, a landscape of magical perfumes where I lost myself for a while and lingered, so that it would never come to an end.

Even today, I remain forbidden before such wonders.

That morning, I let the uncertain dance of my hands quiver on her skin, making delicate and slow paths with my fingertips. I kept caressing her thick hair, a velvety feeling, fascinated by the red color with its sinuous gray highlights. My exploration began at her temple and forehead, then wandered somewhere behind her shoulder. Flustered by the weight of her breasts, held so snugly beneath the lace, my wide eyes sparkled and took in all the images and secrets her transparent clothing could barely hide. In no time, I fell into a magical world of desire, shapes, curves, scents, electrifying shivers down my spine, and all these new words, odes, and songs.

Had I known her better, I would certainly have noticed the delicate movements out of the corner of her eye. She savored every tiny inch of pleasure, enjoyed the awkward but sincere joy I was giving her. Her half-closed eyes almost allowed a glimpse of the incandescence of two star-filled skies. No longer asleep, she left me to do my thing so as not to intimidate me and to prolong the intensity of the moment.

We woke up at the same time, still intoxicated, as if we had just been roused from a dream, stunned, lost in never-before-explored places. Enlivened by the ambivalent feelings only forbidden lovers know, surprised at having done the irreparable in sensual pleasure, feeling somewhat uncomfortable and unsure. We had hardly begun to scratch the surface.

Wilfried N'Sondé

Accustomed to misfortune and mistreatment, I might have preferred to curl up into myself. An animal in its cage. Forbid myself to believe, for fear of being disappointed! I had been without love for so long that it was difficult to accept the prospect of being happy. The light bothered me. I had wandered away from happiness for so long that my shadow cast darkness over stars filled with luminosity. I had never given anything a real try for fear of falling short. I had always fled the anxiety of failure.

A kiss on my forehead from Christelle, accompanied by a radiant smile. Tea or coffee?

Something had changed. Until now, I had been living in combat, victory or defeat, conquer or be conquered. Fear and misery had made me cruel, relentless. I functioned automatically in survival mode, no matter the cost!

The hate I carried in me must have been like the color of disgusting bile, an uncontrollable torrent of pain and anguish fused together, a hideous larva, always on high alert. Cunning, it would be asleep when a random bad mood, from an irritation or an old wound that had never been treated, would growl and explode. Impulsive in their movements, ugliness and resentment would destroy everything in my path. Together, they oozed cruelty in my gaze, fed on rancor and tears, every time more abject. This had been my sustenance every day for years on end.

It was on this deep, wide-open wound that Christelle spontaneously placed her caresses, her words, and her smile.

A LITTLE LATER, Christelle went to her room to get ready to go to the hospital. Alone in the living room, I got ready too. When she was finally dressed and ready to leave, Christelle contemplated me in my pathetic getup. A sudden uneasiness filled the room. I did not know what to say. At first, she asked me where I was thinking of going. I spoke vaguely of a shelter for illegal immigrants on the other side of Paris. She squinted, pursed her lips in a regretful smile, and placed her hand on my cheek.

"You can stay here. You must be tired. Relax a little bit; tomorrow, I'll go with you!"

After taking the time to lay a long, firm kiss on my inexperienced lips, she closed the door behind her.

As she started down the stairs, the euphoria began to fade. Turmoil and confusion began to cloud Christelle's thoughts. How could she go away and leave all that she possessed to the mercy of a total stranger? Leave in his care her little two-room apartment, kitchen, bathroom, toilet, for which she had dragged her meager savings and homebuyer's savings plan file from bank to bank to apply for a loan and been turned down each time. She started getting worked up in her head. I had touched her right in the heart and planted a powerful, unfamiliar feeling in the depths of her being. At some point, she probably told herself that she should not still be holding on to ideas about Prince Charming at her age.

I knew only that she had left and had asked me to be here when she got back. Her request beamed in the sparkle of her eyes, a simple and sincere sentence, whispered. And I did not have the words to tell her how much I was suffering in that moment just because I was separated from her.

For her, most men were not worth much, yet she really would have liked to have a man in her life, now more than ever, before she became ugly and old. Christelle was ready to risk everything and live with me beyond the silence of her closed doors and console herself with the idea that, finally, someone was thinking about her and suffering from her absence when she was not there!

To hear at least one time, Darling, I missed you!

No man had ever whispered this in her ear with lips moist with desire!

Christelle pushed open the door to the building . . . Her last folly! As long as I stayed and waited for her and was kind to her!

～

Relieved and surprised, I watched her from the window. She disappeared into the crowd at the bus stop. Not wanting to risk losing anything of her presence, I carefully followed each of her steps, attuned myself to her every stride, never losing sight of the slightest movement of the body that had given so much to me.

～

Unsettled by the night that had just passed, Christelle tried to put her thoughts together. There were moments when she had been ashamed to reveal herself as so naive. Her pulse would beat rapidly when she thought of me! She did her best to organize her thoughts, to avoid getting carried away too quickly. To stay focused. The rhythm of daily work steadied Christelle; it defined her life. Laziness made her anxious. When she was at the hospital, she had the illusion of living by handing her sense of freedom over to others. Her parents had taught her modesty, hang-ups, and the bent posture of those who have resigned themselves. Excuse me, sir; excuse me, madam, I'm really sorry! Restraint and order, take your time, especially to weigh the risks before making a decision.

Christelle would have given anything to drift off in my arms and flee the nights of solitude in front of the television drooling over the lives of others. Cold nights and days of silence in her tidy little apartment.

To avoid having to think too much about it, Christelle buried herself in work.

~

This morning, she walked quickly to cut through the frigid winter wind. Maintaining her determined pace, she strode firm-footed across the sad gray of the concrete. The filthiness of a day that never really awakens. A dull light. Courageously, she braved the monotonous landscape of square buildings. The only ray of sunlight was the meager hope buried within her chest!

Our encounter had taken her out of her anonymity and the morose nature of her small town at the periphery of Paris, where people do not speak to one another and everyone is bogged down in debt and bills. Not to mention the cups of black coffee without which it all goes wrong. Cigarettes. The rites of boredom that lull the routine, the reassuring habits, an alarm clock that already sounds the end of the day, always too soon, a quick glance out the window, what's the weather like? Hours of life lost on public transportation had already convinced her that she was nothing! Lost in an oppressive Great Whole. She secretly wished that with our mirage of love, everything would finally change, even her fear of getting old that made her feel so fragile and alone.

Wilfried N'Sondé

As she took off for the train station, I recalled the ride we had taken together. The cold and filth of the poor suburbs were even more painful viewed from above.

I was not sure if I had landed in hell or in paradise. A new place, foreign. Unbelievable night, confusing thoughts. Was she going to denounce me to the police? My brain did not know how to handle such complicated matters. I had never learned how to understand the complexity of human feelings. I had been functioning merely to survive and take care of my immediate needs.

I reconstructed from memory the features of her face in the mirror, and once the image was complete, a strong, almost painful desire came over me to feel her next to me.

I saw Christelle's clothes lying in a jumble on the floor, with her omnipresent scent. I automatically began to inspect the place.

I let my shoulders relax and plunked myself down on the sofa to relieve myself of the weight of the years.

I plopped myself down as I had never allowed myself to do before, relaxed, and breathed. I was waiting patiently for the maternal breasts, Christelle's words and her attentive ear as she listens to my confessions. In a few hours, she would come through the door, and it would start all over again.

~

After a little while, I looked around for something to keep me busy. First, I tackled the dishes. Without giving it too much thought, I got the vacuum going, fighting against the past that had latched on to me, regrets kept coming back to me in a confused way. The sea of remorse expelled tears of regret. Sweeping away the dust and the whiffs of violence that I knew only too well. Stopping sometimes for a minute or for an hour, wearing a sad expression, seeing over and over again in my head the kaleidoscope of misfortunes.

As usual, I thought of Marcelline, delightful, tenderness and sadness, both of us separated since our childhood. Thanks to information I had gotten from the sergeant in my barracks when I was a militiaman, I knew that she had survived!

Until she was to visit me in my dream, I would have no idea what had become of her after the civil war!

Wilfried N'Sondé

MARCELLINE'S STORY CAME back to me. I glimpsed the magisterial hand of Mother Earth as she lay my sister right beside me to tell me her story.

Once she had healed, life in the village had returned to its usual rhythm. No one missed me. Devastated by her granddaughter's illness, our grandmother Louise realized that she needed to let her guard down and devote her final years to cherishing her granddaughter. Marcelline was even more spoiled and gratified. She had to put up a fight to be able to go school. Afraid that something horrible might happen to her, Louise had preferred to keep her close!

Learn at school, despite the teacher's severity. Marcelline discovered the world of knowledge with a sense of wonder. Studious and disciplined, she performed exceptionally well right from the beginning. As usual, she also delighted her teacher and soon took her place at the top of the class. Although she had to travel several kilometers to get to school, it was not surprising to find her the first student to arrive in the classroom, wise, attentive, patient. She was also the last one to leave and never lost an opportunity to ask yet another question before heading home. Her teacher Nkaya was overjoyed to have a student like her, and he was only too aware of the importance of his commitment to teaching in these isolated rural areas. He was among those who believed in emancipation through learning. Far from all the talk of the theoreticians of the revolution, he lived his convictions in his daily life. He often came to Louise's hut, to ask her to lighten the chores that rural life imposed on Marcelline so that she could devote more time to her studies. In truth, Louise was afraid to see Marcelline going further away in words and books that were foreign to her. Louise would assign useless chores to my sister. The fear of losing her grandchild forever compelled the old lady to keep her as close as possible!

Marcelline excelled to such a degree that Nkaya was sometimes stunned into silence before her increasingly sophisticated and pertinent reflections. He pleaded with her grandmother, in the name of the liberation of women, in light of the surge in third world countries and the favorable outcome of the revolution and universal renewal. The old lady eventually gave in. His arguments went straight to her heart, filled with aspirations from times gone by. She had retired to the life of a hermit, tears dried up, but hope forever alive. Marcelline got into a prominent high school in the capital. A distant aunt offered her a place to stay so that she could complete her studies.

The horizon now seemed radiant for Marcelline; the sky was merciful. All her dreams seemed within reach.

I WAITED FOR Christelle in the warmth of the apartment, and hope was slowly reborn in me. The dishes were done. I had tidied up everything in order to make her happy.

Everything was happening so quickly. I was getting used to being in a new space, I was getting comfortable with my new-found sense of well-being . . . Glancing at the door, listening for the sound of steps in the stairwell. Only yesterday, I was despised; today, here I was, missing someone, my eyes riveted to the front door.

At the hospital, Christelle's day was a disaster. Her patients were disappointed by her distraction and distance. Distress made them sensitive to the slightest change in their environment. They kept calling on her, clamoring for her from the depths of their beds. They were relentless, pressing the buzzer and calling after her. On this particular day, their favorite nurse's aide was not giving them her undivided attention! Her mind was confused and excited all at once. Her life had really and truly been turned upside down. She feared the moment she would return home and open the door. Would I still be there, would

I have taken off, stolen from her? Dream or reality, was it simply an illusion?

~

During her break, she tried to reach out to everybody, but no one answered the telephone. Christelle would have to go it alone and face the situation. Everyone was surprised by how forgetful she was. Over all the years, she had never failed to accommodate everybody.

Now, she existed only to pursue what was going on with me, a lifeline to forgetting the days and nights of crying and self-recrimination, lying alone in her bed with a pain so deep that it swept her into nothingness.

~

Attentive to sounds in the stairwell, I tried to analyze the footsteps I heard and their direction. Doubt. As I was starting to get desperate, I heard the metallic clinking behind the door, keys trying to find their way into the lock. On the other side, Christelle was trembling. From the street, she had already noticed that the light was on in her apartment. The game with the keys felt like an eternity to both of us.

I had wisely stayed and waited for her!

Christelle pushed open the door. Her knees wobbled, her cheeks were purple, and tears welled up in her eyes. Overwhelmed, images and a multitude of desires flooded into her head. I stood facing the front door.

Christelle kissed me. She fell into my open arms, and we stayed like that, holding each other, surprised and excited to be together. We were tenderly riding the wave of our desire to be together.

~

In my chaotic heart, which had been resuscitated by Christelle, I imagined a goddess of the World, a feeling of calm and well-being. Her image brought back memories of Marcelline.

In my dream, Marcelline told me her story. I cried profusely. Her story was heartbreaking, and I had not been there to hold her hand, more importantly, to protect her.

When she had moved to the capital, her certainties were still intact. She joined many youth organizations. She was an enthusiastic volunteer, participating in social projects that met the needs of the poor. Unspeakable misery, scrawny children, malnutrition, and chronic shortages of medicine. Hunger, the kind that makes men predators. Her commitment felt like a calling.

Marcelline loved traveling throughout the country, from north to south, with the other girls in her choir. They would go singing happiness, hope, all in the name of God and the revolution. As a soloist, Marcelline shone bright when out of her throat came the highest notes, the most mesmerizing melodies, a true pleasure to the ears of spectators, who were thoroughly won over . . . They tried very hard to believe in the unity of the nation.

Yet on some nights, a trained ear could clearly hear the grinding of teeth. Resentment. The evil-eyed, those who denied differences, monsters who preferred to destroy rather than construct.

～

Marcelline maintained an unshakable faith. She financed her schooling by working as a vendor in the market so as not to be a burden to anyone and support her grandmother back in the village.

Everything was going well for her. High school exams were coming up, and she was studying tirelessly, with even greater fervor. Marcelline was dreaming of going to medical school, white coat, stethoscope hanging down, surrounded by the faces of people who were happy and grateful for the care she provided. Following the example of her former teacher, she wanted to work in rural areas, where needs were most urgent. At that time, money was not important to Marcelline; she wanted to be useful.

To avoid disruptions from the frequent power cuts in a country that was gradually falling apart, she often went to the airport with her classmates while preparing for her exams, where enormous floodlights lit the runways all night long. A month before her first exam, in philosophy, cargo aircraft landed with mysterious cases that military personnel off-loaded and immediately hid away. Soldiers wielding machine guns prohibited the high school students from hanging around the area, classified information.

When she was finally ready, all the course material memorized and feeling pretty confident, a gust of flames followed by a downpour of shells came crashing down on her neighborhood.

Cadavers in the streets, assassins, rape in broad daylight. The traumatizing sound of a bomber aircraft, two helicopters! Once they had passed through, nothing but desolation and ruins, smoldering ashes and blood everywhere. Run. In a panic, Marcelline walked to the village to take refuge at her grandmother's home with her books and folders! In the jungle, hunted night and day by a bloodthirsty murderous regime, drugged and famished, she held on to her convictions and kept studying. Even when others began to imagine death as a way out, given that life was simply burying them in mud and horror, Marcelline refused to give up.

After several months of wandering in the jungle, Marcelline joined the living dead, who surrendered to the victors. From these half-starved spectral figures, exhausted, with deeply marked features and empty expressions, militiamen took their only remaining possessions, hope and dignity. One sergeant, a young boy, ripped up her books and notebooks and generously distributed them to his comrades in arms, who used them as toilet paper. During the horrors of civil war, the troop's hygiene was more important than knowledge! Taken into the care of European NGOs, many refugees died, unable to relearn how to properly nourish themselves. Marcelline survived.

Isolated in the devastated capital, shattered by the shock of the war, she started searching for her former classmates. She managed to reunite with about ten or so. Together, they decided to pay their teachers themselves, to ensure that their classes would continue. For several months, no one had received a salary. These young people did not shy away from illegal activity to earn the amounts required for their education. Prostitution was trivialized. Survival no longer had anything to do with the weight of morality. For everyone, it was simply a matter of cold, hard logic.

Money was a real issue; it became an obsession at every single turn and affected every single human relationship in the long run. Love and friendship became superfluous and uninteresting!

Marcelline succeeded in getting her high school diploma, with distinction, in the sciences. But after the hostilities, our country came to a standstill. Then it regressed. It was surviving on a drip and could offer Marcelline nothing but the prospect of wasting away. Years of destruction and impunity had killed the desire to build. Executioners and victims alike looked at each other menacingly. Any movement forward was neutralized. An unbearable tension pressed dangerously on the disillusionment and misery. Huge black clouds of frustration and anger cast a shadow over the future.

Like the overwhelming majority of our compatriots, Marcelline was caught up in the frenzy to get away, escape this impasse at all costs, and head for the Eldorado to the north.

MARCELLINE ARRIVED IN Paris with a heavy heart, weighed down by lies and her clandestine status. She found lodgings with a distant cousin and did everything she could to forget about the horrors of the war. Pessimism and existential doubt would have been a fatal luxury for her. No time for qualms. A friend of our aunt's rented Marcelline her ID, and she was able to get a job.

Marcelline soon began to experience a sense of hope. She got her own apartment. And even while she battled the ghosts of the past, her horizons began to open up, and she started getting used to a new life.

The love of a man would surprise her and take her into a maelstrom that would turn out to be cruel.

Only much later would Marcelline learn that the very charming Stanislas Kouyou was the proud possessor of the regrettable moniker Great Stalin. A long-standing illegal immigrant, he had never worked a day in his life. His studies had ended in the ninth grade, and not with a master's in classical literature from the Sorbonne, as he had claimed in his lofty French. Marcelline wept in vain, her bank accounts were frozen, the bailiffs had seized all they could of her possessions, and she was forced to vacate the apartment she was so fond of within a week. Why had the spirits once again remained silent, leaving her to drown in the sordid abyss in which she found herself with Stanislas?

There was hatred in her eyes when she recalled their first meeting.

On that day, she was running the cash register at the fast-food restaurant La Caille up in the twentieth arrondissement. As if it were yesterday, she could still hear the nonsense that used to come out of the mouth of that idiot, her boss, Roland, banging on about how cute she looked as she tried to concentrate on her tasks. He had been all admiration and attentiveness from the moment he had let out soft "ah"s before hiring her. The whole team at the restaurant looked at him with disgust, fawning over the new hire, who had the nerve to remain modest and timid rather than take advantage of his feelings. Marcelline was very grateful to him for this first job because he had finally gotten her out of her illegal work status and her precarious situation. It was true that the ID papers she was using were not hers, but the salary, some of which she was sending back home, was certainly earned by the sweat of her brow. When she had found herself standing in front of Roland for that first interview, she had been overcome by intense nausea. A red face, black and gray hairs sprouting from his most likely poorly washed pale skin. All around him, the nasty stench of greasy food. She would have much preferred to sleep with the devil wandering around from the beginning of time on his way to hell than to imagine herself lying beneath this chubby, potbellied creature with stumps for legs who was most likely not even circumcised!

Love had struck her like a thunderbolt when her eyes met Stanislas's gaze. He had just paid for a cool draft beer, thank you very much, miss! And his coy expression went straight to her heart, along with his predatory smile, his lower lip drooping toward the right. Marcelline immediately noticed his carefully manicured hands, long fingers adorned with nails shaped to perfection. Not to mention the way he carried himself, a noble bearing, assured but in no way arrogant. He had the air of a young boy. Light blue shirt, elegant, dark brown British-style moccasin, washed-out jeans to give the whole outfit a relaxed look . . . Marcelline found herself dreaming.

An uncontrollable tingling wave traveled down her spine and lodged itself in her belly, giving her a pleasant kind of pins-and-needles sensation. It then settled in her chest and intensified at the very tips of her breasts. Marcelline now found herself caught in a thousand hesitations. Her blood was burning white-hot, the glass got away from her. Careful now, sweetie! An employee giggled, Roland forgives her everything! It's OK, miss, Stanislas smiled, and placed his hand on the shoulder of his future conquest. Something contracted just below my poor sister's belly. She did not know what to think anymore. Images paraded before her eyes in which she was tasting the brick color of this man's skin. For her, he had the ideal complexion. All the women in her village would have given in to such charm.

Settled in about two meters from the cash register, Stanislas was immersed in a beautiful edition of *The Sorrows of Young Werther*. A fairy-tale image of a young man with refined manners soaking up German romanticism in the middle of a noisy restaurant and the constant racket of the Rue des Pyrénées. He had to be the reincarnation of the angel of beauty.

～

The Great Stalin spent his days seducing the ladies, going on dates, being invited to dinners or lunches. No one knew where he lived, who his father was, who his mother was, let alone if he had children. His flirtatious eyes made hearts melt in seconds, the time it took for him to transform into an angry monster with a remarkably violent fist. With great skill, he ruined his mistresses. As if the gifts they showered on him were not enough, he would help himself to their checkbooks and credit cards.

What do girls dream about? Stanislas had no idea! As a matter of fact, he did not even give it a thought! All he knew was that they could not resist him, in cafés, nightclubs, the streets, the metro, everywhere and anywhere! All he had to do was simply bring his face into the spotlight of their eyes, and it was pretty much a done deal.

The love machine. That air of the timid child, a lost expression in his almond-shaped eyes, and especially the uncontrollable quivering of his lips, powered a real arsenal of seduction. Behind the mask was the cold assurance of his routine, a near-mathematical calculation of habit. He charmed with the ferocity of a predator.

It had been far too long since his heart had gone wild from a first encounter. His hands had become expert at intimate caresses. Stanislas was virtually his own high-technology industry of orgasms; it was his veritable pride and joy. His sturdy and hot virility, a veteran in all the rhythms and games aimed at fine-tuning what he called the ultimate program. Stanislas, "Stan" to his victims, bragged about having a PhD in love. He embraced women with the intensity of a top athlete. His tender words, his tears, and the pleasure he conveyed, so many different ways of solidifying his performances.

~

Anger and revenge, sisters in managing broken hearts, reared up in Marcelline's stomach as she suffered atrociously. Rage and affliction oozed from her soul. In her imagination, they took the form of two magnificent celestial dogs, beautiful and swift, who charged out and hunted down Stanislas in his nocturnal slumber. These invisible predators discharged all of Marcelline's bitterness into her former lover's chest. Together, they danced and writhed in his nightmares. Frothing at the mouth, they woke Stanislas with a jolt and made respite impossible. He had a hard time screaming, these blue and silver dogs pinned him to the bed in the middle of the day for hours on end. Immobilized, he was left to examine the white ceiling in his room.

His friends began to worry upon seeing his neglected appearance, hearing his incoherent speech.

In the depths of her dying heart, Marcelline no longer had either the strength or the beauty to disregard negative feelings. She had never consciously wished for the death of this man who had hurt and deceived her so much. Although he was exhausted, Stanislas nevertheless mysteriously managed to throw himself under a truck and gave up the ghost!

~

Marcelline was busy putting the pieces of her life back together. From time to time, to save herself from sinking into madness, she thought about the nights of our childhood.

~

What is the point of falling, getting up, and sinking again? The world around her was indifferent to her disarray. To the solitude, her frustrated hopes. Her fighting spirit had left her. Marcelline wanted to go home; even if it meant she would die, she would at least have the presence of our ancestors and the landscape of our laughter. This new land wanted nothing to do with her or, for that matter, her expectations, which were still so simple. In despair, she went to the police.

At the police station, the officer who saw her crying brought her into an office to talk with her privately.

~

"I've been living in France illegally for some time now," she said. "I've been working with fake papers, please send me back to my country, I no longer want to live on the fringes of the law!"

Surprised and touched at the same time, the policeman told her to calm down.

❧

Had she been a victim of mistreatment?

❧

She wanted to go back home!

He could protect her. Marcelline did not know how to explain to him that everything she held dearest was at risk of falling apart. She wanted to go back home! She was an honest woman who had been trampled by disillusion. The civil servant encouraged her, noticing how well she spoke French. She would not have problems integrating, she could benefit from the support of her compatriots. Marcelline insisted that she wanted to go back home!

With a paternal hand on her shoulder, he begged her to hang in there. The policeman knew an organization that could counsel her and help her. The war was still going on in her country!

The exchange with the police officer left her confused. Marcelline was at the end of her rope, but after their long meeting, she seized this last opportunity. She left the police station with an address scribbled on a piece of paper in her handbag. One last chance. A feeble glimmer of hope, the meager prospect of a solution.

Wilfried N'Sonde

MY NAME IS Henriette Mpessé. I grew up in the village with my parents and my six brothers. At the age of twelve, when the civil war had just broken out, militiamen showed up one night looking for enemies on the run whose uniforms they had found discarded on the path leading to our home. They violently brought us all out of our huts and gathered us in the big square. Our old chief tried to calm them down; they executed him. The militiamen pillaged, and they killed my father in front of us with blows from their rifle butts. Three of them began to rape my mother, who fell unconscious. When my brothers tried to intervene, they sprayed them with bullets. As for me, they raped me and beat me all night long, all of them drunk. I never found out what they were looking for. Left to die, it was the pain in my body and soul that woke me up in the early morning. We were but seven survivors. We fled, for fear that the militiamen would return. Our family members were left out in the rain to rot, without proper burial, for scavengers to feast on. I returned to the capital, where my aunt put me up. She's a good Christian; she really took care of me. I helped her with her business in the market where she had a stand selling print fabric.

Policemen came demanding money every day because they themselves were never paid on time. The amount they asked for kept going up. My aunt and I went to complain to the senior district officer. He seemed understanding, wrote everything down, and assured us that he would take care of it as soon as possible. That same night, about ten police officers, dressed in plainclothes, this time, forcibly entered our parcel. My aunt was immediately killed with a bullet to the head. They forced her husband to rape me in front of them before killing him with kicks to the head. What they did to me afterward I'd prefer to talk about in a private interview. I was incarcerated for six months, beaten and raped every day. One of the wardens, originally from my village, took pity on me. I agreed to tell him where my aunt had hidden her savings, so he helped me escape from the prison and obtained a passport for me. Thanks to that, I was able to make it to Charles de Gaulle airport. Today, I suffer from terrible pains in my lower abdomen.

I am persecuted by horrific nightmares. I cannot return to my country, I'm wanted for having escaped. My first application for asylum was rejected because I had no proof. They basically threw me in prison without a hearing or a judgment, incarcerated arbitrarily. There is not one trace of paperwork, not even a file about my case. I'm begging you, ladies and gentleman, to reconsider my request.

～

My name is Clotaire Ngoulou. I was a member of the Special Forces in my country . . . At the end of the civil war, my regime remained hidden in the bush . . . I got wind of abuses within certain sections of my unit. As an officer, I led an investigation . . . Agents of the Secret Service asked me to put a stop to the procedure. I persevered because I love the army in my country; it is our national pride. Honor is an essential value for me. These brutes came to my home during my absence to rape my wife and

Wilfried N'Sondé

two daughters . . . I was beaten up, tortured, buried up to the neck so that my head would be exposed to direct sunlight and rain. They piled twelve of us into a cell of just fifteen square meters. Humiliation and torture, daily. To escape, I had to offer my body to the chief warden of the prison. I was able to make it to Belgium . . . To France . . . It's impossible for me to return to my country, I'm a wanted man there!

⌒

This was about the tenth such statement Laurent Levasseur had read that afternoon. He thinks to himself that in an extremely poor society rife with violence, the prison environment must be the place that most resembles hell.

He had been asked to immerse himself in the reality of the cases that needed to be examined. As a law student, he had chosen to work voluntarily for this organization that helps refugees. He was happy to complement his theoretical education with real work experience, not to mention the pleasure of knowing that he was being useful. Laurent, an only child from a respectable family, had never wanted for anything. In his cramped office without air conditioning, with horrible seating, he was beginning to suffer, twisting constantly on his chair with a sharp pain between his shoulder blades. His buttocks were also hurting. It was becoming more and more difficult to concentrate.

⌒

The militiamen showed up, smoking drugs and reeking of booze . . . raped the women, executed the men with a bullet to the nape of the neck . . . Some were laughing . . . using the heads as soccer balls.

⌒

Laurent systematically massaged the bridge of his nose. To stay awake, he turned on the coffee machine. All these stories were beginning to sound the same and become somewhat boring.

~

... It cost me a lot of money to buy a passport from a French national in my country to dupe the immigration officers ...

~

As he was blowing his nose and becoming more and more distracted, his gaze fell on a beautiful girl sitting in the bus station on the other side of the road. Weary of the horrific stories and tormented by the suffocating heat, Laurent gladly ogled the dreams that the miniskirt and half-opened legs were barely hiding. Daydreaming for a few seconds, he imagined himself crossing the street to go talk to her ...

~

... We spent six months in the jungle eating nothing but dirt and roots. Children no longer cried. As soon as they could no longer walk, they closed their eyes, collapsed, and died, their skin became one with the earth. We would take off heading for nowhere.

~

Intrigued by the girl's considerable breasts, Laurent secretly wished that one of the straps of her tank top would give out or that by some strange miracle her miniskirt would just disappear. However challenging it was, he tried to chase away the images of his face lost between her breasts or intoxicated from the moisture between her legs.

~

At about the same time, Marcelline was coming out of the metro entrance on her way to her appointment. Still amazed by her meeting with the police officer, she regretted not having kissed him to thank him. Convinced that once again the spirits of our ancestors had sent her a sign, assured of her footing, she headed toward her destiny. She was aware that it was important to simply follow the message and allow events to unfold, however inexplicable, because it was not about logic, it was about a force.

The spirits surrounding Mother Earth were not speaking to her; they were guiding her according to a unique sequence of events.

Marcelline had not had any trouble memorizing the address. She made her way to the headquarters of the charity organization for refugees, her last chance for a decent life. On the telephone, the person in charge had been very comforting, reassuring her in a sweet and sincere voice that she would be in good hands. She had nothing to worry about. She had not been able to sleep through the night, even though her spirits were pretty high. She kept imagining how the meeting would go. She had better not forget anything! Refreshed and in the best mood after her morning shower, she had taken the time to shave her underarms and use deodorant. There was no way she was going to show up in a white man's office smelling like an animal or with embarrassing sweat stains under her arms. Marcelline also made sure her underwear was new. She knew she was capable of fainting in the face of a major disappointment, and they would most likely have to undress her to revive her . . . You do not get to keep your dignity if it turns out you're wearing questionable underwear!

～

. . . If for some reason I were to return to my country, there is absolutely no doubt that I would immediately be eliminated. In fact, I'm a problematic witness because I was in a militia and committed crimes in the name of the regime that is still in power. I fled to save my life. I'm seeking political asylum in France.

～

On that note, and with a deep sigh of relief, Laurent Levasseur finally closed the files. He wiped his forehead, perhaps to wipe away the doubts that were beginning to pile up. He felt powerless before all these tragedies and horrors. Certain testimonies even sounded exaggerated. Across the way, the bus carried away the breasts and half-baked fantasy, probably off to some idiot and a life to which he would never have access. What a waste! A quick glance at his watch, he had just enough time to freshen up before enduring the story of the asylum seeker whom he was about to receive.

⮑

Marcelline had spent hours trying to decide on the most appropriate attire for the occasion. In the end, jeans, a T-shirt, and sneakers had won out. Dressed this way, she felt relatively at ease, despite the indescribable stress squeezing her stomach. A suit seemed too elegant, more likely to produce an image that contradicted the distress an illegal immigrant should embody. My sister held her file almost too close to her chest. Her fingers were trembling; she was gripped by the desire to finally live, papers in order, a job . . . Happiness.

⮑

There were three gentle knocks at Laurent's door. Bladder emptied, face freshened up, a cup of hot coffee steaming on the well-organized table, he was ready to listen. Ready to lead his first interview.

Expecting to see war, rape, human misery, a squadron of ghostlike, bloodthirsty militiamen drunk, drugged, he was speechless, stunned when Marcelline entered. She came in, her head tilted slightly but with the direct, luminous, determined expression of someone in search of a hand extended to save her.

⮑

When he saw her come in, Laurent was impressed by her silhouette, her elegance, and her thin, endless legs. He remained fixated on her thick, dark lips, shaped to perfection. He also appreciated her high cheekbones, not to mention the long, harmonious line from her hands to her neck. Her skin, with its beautiful brown complexion, sparkled, amazing with her full figure. His gaze drowned in Marcelline's immense, black, magical eyes, her freshly braided hair, pulled back to show her face, giving her an air of grace and nobility.

Attracted to Marcelline's body, Laurent asked a number of evasive questions. Touched, Marcelline described her situation with courage and modesty. Despite her efforts, she did not always give accurate answers. Her memory kept selecting what she could recall. Attentive and patient, Laurent quickly won her confidence. Once she felt reassured, Marcelline revealed more of herself. He listened for long periods without interrupting her. He also proved to be very gentle and gallant in order to please the young lady. She left feeling extremely grateful and happy that the organization had given her case to a man who was so understanding. She gladly returned to see him.

After several interviews, Marcelline noticed that his interest in her went way beyond a professional relationship. Each time she looked away, his focus was primarily on her chest and the curve of her back. This heavy and persistent gaze, which she could feel following her each time, bothered her a lot.

To see her more often, he would ask her to come by the office, under the pretext that he needed more details about her story or additional documents to strengthen her case. Tenacious and determined, Marcelline confided the details of her roller-coaster life to him. She tried to persuade him with her gentlest voice, to soften him with tears that she could not hold back when she related some of the most sordid episodes of her life.

One day, as she was sobbing while remembering the war, Laurent coldly looked her straight in the eye; he wanted to invite her to dinner and take her to bed! Shocked, Marcelline suddenly straightened up.

Aside from her love for me, Marcelline had experienced only deception and suffering with men. Now here was a young student with a lecherous gaze asking for her body in exchange for his help, her last resort for getting back on her feet and improving her situation. She answered:

"I have other things to do. I didn't come here for that. I've suffered, I've known hunger and horrors. I've come within inches of death, and even when I look at other human beings, it's as if death has turned its back on me and walked away."

~

Tired of resisting, she ended up accepting his invitation. He had insisted so much, and, in any case, why turn down a good meal? Furthermore, there had been so many lies and mistakes in her life thus far that she was a terrible judge of character; in the same way, she had a hard time with her overall vision of the world, which had been so badly distorted.

Marcelline let herself be desired and knew above all that he would do everything to help her. It was now more a matter of not disappointing him. Thanks to this man, she would get the papers she so desperately needed. Love, love, something had broken in her, now she knew how to be calculating to get her needs met.

~

Love and desire, she had probably left them behind in the hut in the village that I had left, fleeing anathema. Marcelline had a broken heart; her dreams had been shattered, maybe forever.

~

Laurent's constant caresses annoyed her, and his tongue wrapped around hers disgusted her. The problem was that she had to put up with this to get what she needed. Marcelline let him unleash his desire in her, two or three times in complete darkness. In these moments, Laurent would become hysterical, telling her he had never loved like this before, that she was like a hallucinogenic. He was a slave to her curves and contours, which he compared to mountains and valleys to climb and tumble down until he was exhausted, especially the black plain extending out from her belly, not to mention her hands and her mouth. He would caress her for long periods, fascinated by the small of

Wilfried N'Sondé

her back, sculpted in the shape of the letter S. He could never give her up.

Wild, he would hold her passionately. Tossed about with intensity—he turned her, twisted her, shook her every which way on his bed—Marcelline would moan along with him until Laurent took off far away into the sphere of ecstasy. After he had cried in pleasure like a man who had never had an orgasm before, he would collapse next to her, drained, breathless, consumed . . . Alone!

～

While Laurent lay next to her, Marcelline wiped herself. She cleaned her skin, mechanical movements, with the greatest care, clean and conscientious like when we were children. Then she modestly pulled her nightgown down over her knees and covered her buttocks. Filled with contempt, she turned away and showed him her back.

～

"You're amazing. I've never made love like that!"

～

Strangely calm, Marcelline worked hard to forget most of all the noises and images of war embedded in her memory. She painstakingly chased away the wandering phantoms from the cemetery weighing on her chest.

Marcelline gathered up the taste of my tongue somewhere on her shoulder, the sensation of her childhood. A strong light from the equatorial dawn, hot and humid, just before the storm. Having paid dearly for her survival, cost what it may, she fell asleep with a strained smile . . . Heart and soul broken, hope shattered!

Once she received her ten-year residence permit, thanks to Laurent's efforts, Marcelline stopped seeing him. She kept a low profile. Absent, she took refuge in a parallel universe that was invisible and pure.

In the solitude of her retreat, she often called upon the kindness of Nzambi A Mpoungou, Mother Earth of all that can and cannot be seen, to carry her into a comforting bath with gentle, round, protective breasts. The goddess warmed her defiled body in this way.

For the wounds of her heart, Marcelline called upon the creator of the rivers, tears, and winds to bring her to me so that she could rediscover the pleasure of my presence, running hand in hand until we were completely out of breath and no longer on the main paths. Not to mention the touch of my moist lips. A sensation of smooth velvet on her shoulder that would spread everywhere all over her skin. Enraptured in a hypnotic fire, a glimmer forever inscribed in our memory . . .

~

In my dream, Marcelline had lost the carefree nature she used to have when she let herself go wholeheartedly, laughing, eyes beaming with innocence. Only when she thought of me did she have enough in her to love.

MINUTES, HOURS HAD gone by, night was falling. Christelle and I had brought up, however reluctantly, the shelter for illegal immigrants, where I should turn myself in tomorrow morning. We both would have preferred to defer my departure indefinitely, but neither one of us could imagine an alternative solution. We were simply glad to be able to extend the connection born from our first glances on the train. We continued along on a tightrope, careful but at the same time thirsting for openness and curiosity, eager to be able to reveal ourselves without restraint and to allow each other to say what we really wanted to say. Trust in each other intensified from one moment to the next. Christelle and I discovered the euphoria that came with completely confiding in each other.

A warm, intimate, and yet chaste relationship gradually developed. The bond we shared was modest and full of gratitude, but there was also some turmoil. Our bodies shared an intense sensuality that was quieted by our gestures. An amicable, furtive, tender kiss had confused us. The lingering of my inexperienced hand on Christelle's back quickly transformed into a caress. I affectionately smoothed her fly-away hairs back in place. Pleasantly surprised, she held back the relief she felt and repressed a smile. We had become so close to each other, each inundated by the other's scent, that our composure became a strange form of exciting torture. And when she could read the desire in my glances, Christelle would taste the confusion of her senses, whimsical, eager, a flood of saliva would fill her mouth, and her lower abdomen would drown in moisture.

Deep down, we enjoyed this game of suffering and keeping each other at a good distance, especially Christelle, who was so accustomed to the frivolity of men. With me, Christelle was slowly reconciling with herself, but this time she wanted to take her time and let her body and her soul open up together, at the same time. She was fighting tooth and nail against the fear of being deceived yet again by a man.

As for me, I kept hesitating to take her and make passionate love to her. Careful not to break the amazing moment together and destroy our shared sensitivities, I waited.

~

According to Christelle, it just felt good being with me, plain and simple. I caught her looking at me, preoccupied, with glistening eyes that gave the impression she was about to burst into tears. Since my sister, Marcelline, no one had ever shown me this much attention. I was so surprised, almost uncomfortable. No one had been interested in me. My life had been a journey from one disaster to the next, an annoying fall into mud, the sounds of war, of fire and metal, living endlessly in panicked fear, and tortured by the uncertainties of the future. My heart and soul had been broken since childhood. When I had arrived in Christelle's modest apartment, I was on my last legs, downtrodden.

The anxiety deep within my chest was fading away in the starry light shining from her green eyes as they crossed mine. In that moment, I was leaving behind the vestiges of misfortune and the reflexes of a wounded wild animal who was always on high alert.

⁓

Christelle was intriguing to me. I was beginning to devote myself to her. It was true. It felt like a cult, almost religious. To me, she was inaccessible, mysterious, fascinating.

Convinced that everything with her should be different, I was getting used to our chaste and tender hours. I felt a long-awaited happiness, finally right within reach.

⁓

Christelle asked me many questions about my childhood and the militia. Her curiosity grew along with the increasingly frequent questions. I dodged some of them, careful to restrict my answers to faint dark shadows, not quite lies, but not fully exposing everything either. As time went on, my hesitation saddened Christelle. She reassured me that she had no desire to judge me or condemn me. She was offering good faith and trust. She wanted us to continue the extraordinary momentum that we had begun when we met.

I had suffered a lot, and that had touched her, but I had also been somewhat vague about episodes in the civil war, and she did not quite understand everything; there were details missing, and Christelle desperately wanted to learn more about my superior during that time, the terrible Admiral Rambo. Nothing would stop her, she was determined to understand me better and, to my great dismay, help me.

I would have given anything to forget and for her to never know what I had really done. Her eyes beseeched me. Couldn't she simply think about the present and build a future with me? Christelle wanted to know everything, every last detail of that period of my life, the truth. I was asking her to appreciate the new man that she was going to make of me, but the questions were going around in her mouth, in her eyes, kept cascading down!

Seeing her torment, I became afraid. In spite of myself, my old reflexes crept back. I became quiet and closed myself off in my shell. I vacillated between silence and the desire to be sincere, prayed to Mother Earth so that Christelle would forgive my unspeakable crimes.

~

She began to cry her eyes out, sitting on the floor, her chin resting on her knees as her stiff arms hugged her bent legs tightly to her chest, her hair disheveled. The face that I loved so much was ravaged; from under swollen, red eyelids, her green eyes interrogated me.

I felt a violent pang in my heart. I swore to myself that I would do whatever it took for her to regain the gentle, tranquil, magnificent momentum of our first evening.

I took her hands in mine and plunged into the story that I would have preferred to forget!

ONCE I FLED the village, I reached the capital, bathed in light. I was overcome by the big city, its river and tributaries. It wore its name proudly, the green heart of Africa, its streets filled with intense activity, animated by a crowd in unshakably good spirits. Children were laughing and playing in the inner courtyards. A joyous capital, women smiling, babies on their backs. This playful city with its elegant dandies, dapper men in outfits composed with precision, down to the last detail, flaunting a sophisticated gait and a mannered, often killer, turn of phrase in their speech. The music was equally seductive and could be heard at street corners while drinking a beer. Not to mention the beautiful alleyways between whitewashed brick houses. Bars where people could dance all night long and that never emptied before dawn. Alcohol flowed freely, the dark eroticized eyes of men and women wrapped in each other's arms as they moved slowly with their backs arched, on the dance floors! The symbol of an independent country that had finally been transformed into an open and tolerant space. It was time to move forward, make progress. The women were the real soul of the city. They had an essential role, were the sovereign rulers of the markets. By day, they provided food items and daily necessities, and by night, they used their culinary talents to feed the population of the dance bars.

The quality of the infrastructure left a lot to be desired. Little had been built since the colonial authorities had departed. The capital superimposed new structures on buildings conceived for other purposes. We were forever screaming "modernity" at the top of our lungs, all the while holding firmly to tradition. In truth, everyone was playing with what it meant to him or her. Opportunism became the order of the day, enjoy life, get drunk, and party.

Abandoned by their elders, youngsters like me did not understand what was going on, and our concerns went unanswered. We were disruptive; the capital was pulsating to a festive rhythm.

In the beginning, I was a street kid. I was dirty. My body was covered with infected sores, and my skin was a disgusting mix of dust and sweat. All day long, I roamed the streets barefoot under the implacable sun, especially in the city center or around the airport. There, I followed European tourists and tried to sell them anything I could, sunglasses, peanuts, or American cigarettes. Sometimes I even offered my scrawny body in exchange for a warm meal, a shower, or the possibility of sleeping in a real bed.

My nights I spent in fear, sleeping anywhere, in a cardboard box or a stolen blanket, always surrounded by the stench of the garbage they would burn because they did not know how else to get rid of it. With no garbage collection service, filth was ubiquitous, in the streets, in the inner courtyards, by the rivers where housewives washed their clothes. On rainy days, the entire city was buried in grime; the streets vomited a black river of mud and trash.

The paved roads represented the reliable portion of the road system. The funds assigned for their construction dried up regularly, often prematurely, in mysterious ways.

I stole and begged at the risk of my life. Later, I was able to join the Dynamic Forces of the Nation, which spearheaded the avant-garde revolution against colonialist conspiracy, international imperialism, and bigwig capitalists! This is where I learned to read and write and where my mind was distorted by Marxist-Leninist principles. For my friends and me, it was about having two shirts, a pair of shorts, a scarf, a machine gun, and a pair of shoes. We received two meals of rice with peanut sauce every day, a piece of boiled beef on Sundays, discipline in the service while giving the nod to comrades Mao, Lenin, Kim Il Sung, Tito, and many others whose names I have long forgotten.

I stood out right away with my engagement in the fist fighting operations! I was particularly effective at hunting down and humiliating opponents, especially women. I was young, frustrated, and vindictive. I even frightened my comrades in arms. They would complain to the sergeant in our barracks. One of them dared to claim I was a monster who needed to be eliminated by a witch doctor or an exorcist-priest!

Sergeant Cesar Nkouffi, the highest-ranking officer, proud of his military training in the Cuban and Soviet academies, of his discipline, rationality, and asceticism as a matter of principle in the service of the proletarian revolution, made preparations. After a detailed inquiry, he was able to prove the authentic birth of Clovis Nzila in the commune of Lingolo with an official duplicate administrative certificate, mother, schoolgirl; father, unknown.

The one who had dared criticize his most effective asset in terms of interrogations, who excelled in the art of squeezing out all sorts of confessions from dissidents by whatever horrific means necessary, was accused of reactionary sentiments, treason, and rebellion and shot without a trial!

I had some good times in the army. It was a dream universe for me. Three solid meals a day. Accustomed to horrible bullying since birth, I did not experience the mistreatment we were subjected to as suffering. As a matter of fact, I had occasion to enjoy my viciousness and fully appreciate the terrifying satisfaction that came from exercising power over others . . .

Weapon in hand, I was finally feared and respected. The eyesore of the village was finally upright, daring and severe in his khaki attire, parading in the streets of the capital wearing a serious and menacing expression. The masses took charge of punishing thieves by lynching them. We were happy to patrol and intimidate, authorized by the impunity we as soldiers had inherited from the coercive colonial authority.

～

No one dared to raise a voice in my presence. Not one hand was raised to bring me down. Thanks to my reputation, women frequently made eyes at me. Clovis Nzila existed.

～

Unfortunately for me, a wall fell somewhere in Europe, people were liberated, and, as has happened for centuries, Africa was called upon to respond as quickly as possible. The shock wave caught us by surprise below the equator, yet another calamity for which neither my country nor I was prepared.

～

It was time again for big changes. We had to catch up with the rest of the planet, fall in line with the *do* of democracy. Socialism and other communisms had imploded. The regime heavyweights all over the continent were busy organizing large-scale national conferences with a huge media presence and eminent foreign observers.

～

Meanwhile, my country was slipping backward, on the verge of collapse. The regime's top brass was still driving around in heavy-duty German vehicles, while hundreds, thousands of young people like me, with nowhere to live, no jobs, and no money, roamed the filthy, dilapidated streets aimlessly. We made up a new race, dehumanized, unloved, raised on belt beatings, bullying, slaps, the middle finger bopping us on top of the head as though that were a hug.

My life had never been worth much, daily reprimands, verbal abuse heaped on me along with humiliation, beatings, my head and gaze kept down. Two arms, two legs to get me about from morning to night, and my trap kept shut!

From the cradle, I was thirsty for blood and vengeance. I am of that generation whose birthright is to keep on going till the breaking point, terrified of curses and anything our parents come up with to spread ignorance and submission. Tradition?

"Tradition" is the word they use to make us feel guilty and to lobotomize my angry brothers and me. We kept going, evil eye, empty stomachs.

We haunted the streets. In truth, the whole continent was standing on its head and left a huge hole in the education and hearts of its countless youth. Nothing coherent was transmitted. Adolescents were developing in an environment made up of heterogeneous elements, gathered randomly from television and video clips. A cacophony of G-strings, Mercedes-Benzes, action movies of the worst quality, and pornography. Indescribable chaos took over where my brain would have been, along with a hunger that could make you fierce and blind, resigned and fatalistic.

During that time, leaders rushed to disguise the misery and irreparableness as democracy. Keep up appearances before it is too late . . . Make up for lost time while it is already too late . . . since . . . some time ago . . . Keep up appearances!

Greedy for money and power, the pro-independence generation had built an unstable government. Keep up appearances . . . show that we are good students. Pretend, cover up what is not working, and whatever you do, do not try to fix the problems or even mention them . . . A sort of continental schizophrenia took over, which confused the spirits . . . Keep up appearances. It's not so bad, that's just the way it is; you can't do much about it . . . Ssshh, don't speak so loudly, someone might hear you! Pretend, in the hope that it will bring peace, but for how much longer? Cross my fellow countrymen every day, look on with utter contempt, and then simply ignore them completely.

Voting was taking place in civilizations where one drives around in a big car, all the streets are paved, surplus food is thrown out or wasted, and the women are whiter and more beautiful. In these countries, nudity is no longer savagery but rather the affirmation of an alternative haute couture, music has no color, one goes to a hospital to get well rather than to die, everybody has electricity and enough running water, and you can die from eating too much. There, where everything is better.

~

The first world was voting, and so we did too. Idle, I was among the first to register to vote. Many of us were secretly hoping to discover the place where the great magic of the white man was hiding, in search of this amazing phenomenon that was supposed to take place at a near-religious moment and that leaves the citizen experiencing the calm and privacy of the voting booth!

Institutes for political analysis began serious investigations. Experts took note of the troubling state of the political parties. Similar to plants that spread rapidly below the equator, parties were proliferating. There was an orgy of academic designations.

A significant number of experts took part in the debates, making it perfectly clear who was situated to the left, to the right, in the center, up, down, in the air! A legion of sans-culottes infected with sexually transmitted diseases was raised in the whorehouses of bad neighborhoods!

Simple minds, full of hope like mine, could no longer keep up.

Simultaneously, a flurry of programs of political one-upmanship arrived on the scene, concocted by a spontaneous generation of men of letters. There were doctors of law, French grammar, sociology, political science, anthropology, tourism ... They had heated discussions in bars and university dining halls, often in front of illiterate electoral bodies who understood nothing.

Hatred became more widespread.

The crisis quietly resisted democracy in the same flippant manner that had allowed it to triumph over communism, torture, and the masters of the invisible world, of the third world, of development and cooperation.

Elections took place all the while the troubles had emptied my belly and consumed my illusions. I had lost so much weight that some were asking themselves if I might not be one of those wild beasts of the past, inadvertently lost in today's country following an unfortunate mystical misunderstanding. In fact, many contested the authenticity of my birth certificate, drawn up by the Lingolo registry service. For the time being, I made a conscious effort to go hungry, and with each step I took, I doubled over in pain, my expression dominated by a cold and piercing gaze. Rain or shine, I wandered barefoot in the dirt, enviously watching the young, happy, and well-fed jet-set crowd. Air-conditioned Mercedes-Benzes, three-piece suits, potbellies, two wives, four mistresses, and legitimate children in Île-de-France. Hundreds of thousands of adolescents sat and waited; their resentment churned accusingly, growing a little louder with each passing day. Jubilant democracy continued. Soon everybody was voting across the board, presidents, ministers, deputies, mayors, village chiefs, prostitutes, soccer players, cooks!

People headed to the polls docile and submissive, hundreds of thousands of men and women without the slightest understanding of proper French. As proof of their new sovereignty, after all the lies of the one-party system, they came to the voting booth and deposited nothing other than the piece of the paper they were not able to read because of their inadequate schooling. Frustrated, they headed back to their neighborhoods and villages.

My generation did not burden itself with complications; it was concerned with surviving, come what may! At the poll where I had taken the opportunity to vote, I had the bad idea of slipping in a foul-smelling, unidentifiable object, to share a moment of my daily existence with the law professors, political commentators, and international dignitaries. They incarcerated me along with all the other troublemakers and released us only after they had given us a good beating.

Indestructible, the bad seed took to the streets again, indifferent to the messages of the ancestors, impervious to the influence of the spirits. Early on, I had learned to ignore the Marxist-Leninist logorrhea, and so it was with democratic verbiage. I had lost my bearings. Drunk on cheap beer. Warped vision, not a dime to my name.

Nzambi A Mpoungou was losing patience. The spirits were worried, love, love!

You could hear the screaming in the distance, tacky, bitter emanations, similar to the excrement of beings as old as the earth. Because of three main problems in the country: breakfast, lunch, and dinner. Mouths stopped speaking and, in concert with the swollen, empty stomachs, set off an uproar. Bad, bad omen.

It made leaders sharpen their weapons . . . More weapons were off-loaded from huge aircraft and then carefully buried near the airport. Tensions were palpable, every day heavier and heavier . . . More weapons, always more weapons. There were firm, uncompromising discussions at the common banquet table concerning oil wealth, numbers, barrels, percentages. The law of the jungle, the best, highway robbery, all monsters! The fiercest protagonist, the multinational company, agitated and jealous, an offended master, he slammed his hand down firmly, a paw ready to claw, on the negotiation table. First of all, a calculation had been made, coldly, scientifically accurate down to the last dollar, economic reasons! Weapons, always more weapons . . .

~

The next day, about ten or so dead bodies were found in the street. At dawn, a morning drizzle. The spirits were numb, taken aback by this picture of chaos. In silence, a crowd gathered in disbelief, dignified and saddened. There are things that speak through their silence, are understood by imagining them. The hammer had struck the anvil heavily with a deafening sound. Dry mouths would perhaps never cry out again. When the shock is too violent, nothing will ever be the same. The bodies of about ten or so young men, still children, were found . . . During the night, they had been savagely assassinated and buried right away. Summarily executed to serve as an example, to intimidate. Cynically, the heads of these adolescents were left jutting above the ground. Apocalyptic image. Horror had most definitely been declared, relentless, irreparable. Ten or more corpses of young adults in the mist of dawn. Heads sticking out of the ground. Blood-streaked testicles in their mouths. Eyes gouged out. Civil war broke out!

CIVIL WAR? ARM Clovis Nzila and the other sad sires of his kind, schoolboys, the unemployed, the nobodies, all the wretched of the earth, and throw a dark veil over the world. Shake up the whole thing brutally, every which way. Create speeches from nothing, each more ridiculous and terrifying than the roaring of a wounded wild animal. Let hatred suddenly rain down on the world. Cook up the most sophisticated torture techniques. In front of incredulous and terrified mothers, pile up the newborns in a mortar with a firm hand, armed with a very solid stick. Let family, love, and friendship perish; achieve total extinction. Then await death, filled with an anxiety in your belly that makes you crazy! Spice up the nights with the stench of terror, looting, and flames. Watch carefully with a camera. Perfume suspicious actions and the bitter taste of settling scores, and throw in cowardice as a bonus. To wrap it all up, cover the sky in silence and a star dimmed by cruelty and despair!

There will be horrific screams from children, from women, from old men, from animals, from men in agony, about the oceans of blood. Civil war.

Purulent, gaping wounds, bright red that will never heal. Mutilated bodies rotting in the streets, runaways skipping over them without blinking an eye, run, keep running. Fingers, legs, breasts, penises, feet, skulls, garlands of organs scattered all over the ground, as though it were the end of the world. Everywhere blood, dirty and black, mixed in with mud. The reality of a naked woman, chained like a dog, delivered with no possible hope of rescue to the sexual deviance of drugged criminals until death delivers her!

It is injustice wearing camouflage, with a helmet of blind and murderous folly, barefoot or shod in plastic sandals, with dirty, ripped shorts. It is a lost adolescent, armed with a Kalashnikov and a penis, transformed into a dangerous outgrowth, destroyer of skins and souls. Civil war. It is the defecation of humanity when men, women, and children have succeeded in healing themselves of any feeling of love. It is beatings with gun butts, bursts of machine-gun fire, a vaccination of a few millimeters of hot lead, launched at record speed, to explode muscles, bones, and gray matter.

Civil war. It is Marcelline, our grandmother, their neighbors, their friends, entire families, men, women, children, old people, a whole population chased into the forest! Panicked, lost in the jungle, having to jump over dead bodies devoured by dogs. Hunted by militiamen drunk and thirsty for killing and sex. It is innocence sleeping in the rain, amid the odors of excrement and urine, after having buried newborn twins to whom life was forbidden, just so that the mother could suffer for one or two weeks more.

Mother Earth, where are your words? Love, love. Confused, the spirits are voiceless, powerless. The legs of children whose empty, swollen bellies explode into a horrifying cry of pain. Women bathe and drink from the same stagnant water.

Runaways no longer slept, they trembled, walking for weeks, a long night of chopped fingers, of severed breasts . . . rape!

Cities burned with their inhabitants. The youth who roamed aimlessly yesterday are militiamen today, finishing off the job with machetes or kicking people to death. Civil war, a massacre fair, where men are lined up against the wall before the death-blow or locked in prisons and systematically sodomized.

Sad to say, among the figures who became renowned for their sophistication in terror was none other than a certain Clovis, renamed Admiral Nzila Rambo!

My singular marine exploit was leaving some poor souls, trying to get to the other side of the river, to drown. I was constantly being told how abnormally ugly I was. My eyes betrayed vindictive pleasure. I terrorized the population as the head of a handful of bloodthirsty demons who had been given unchecked powers, one of which was to help myself to the heart of the population as a means of settling scores. Pillaging and racketeering were institutionalized. We, my lieutenants Lord-of-Death and One-Eye-Two-Words and I, took possession of muscle cars, hi-fis and stereos, chairs, tables, shoes, boxer shorts, and sunglasses.

Lord-of-Death was not even thirteen years old. He killed for fun and proudly wore three feet of barbed wire as a headband in order to impress his enemies.

One-Eye-Two-Words killed because he was wicked and wanted to make the world pay for his double handicap. He was blind in one eye and stammered so much that he preferred not to say anything. He wreaked his vengeance by torturing for no reason, especially children whom he suspected of constantly mocking him. Our victims thought we must have been born to some old female crocodile, especially me. I was accused of having traded my mother's life to some witchdoctors in exchange for this much power. It was impossible to find my birth certificate since, crazed with rage, I had personally burned down the registry office building in Lingolo. I had launched my troops at the city in the hope of finding and saving my sister. But I was too late. She had disappeared!

~

Marcelline, the sole image of beauty and sunlight in my hell, the texture of her skin on the cheek of a child who knew no other tenderness, the taste of her arm on a tiny centimeter at the tip of my tongue. I keep living to have that feeling again from the only person who has ever loved me. When we were children, Marcelline knew how to look past the unsightly layer that covered me.

Christelle and Marcelline are the only ones who can reach deep into me so that I no longer depend on violence toward others as a means of existing.

For so many years, I missed Marcelline—since my solitary flight from our grandmother's village with hate in my heart.

Every day, she had cried for me, even though she knew that my life in the village had been nothing but bullying, violence, and humiliation. Can she imagine the life I have had since then?

~

Stranded in the middle of nowhere, somewhere between heaven and earth, Marcelline and the other runaways sang prayers around a fire. And I and other militiamen searched for them during the night.

~

Today, I regret my mistakes of the past, the hatred for my fellow man. Like everyone else back then, I distrusted my neighbor and was jealous of the well-meaning friend. Fathers envied sons; mothers suspected uncles . . . With the decline of human relations, our society had slipped into complete chaos!

~

With their heads down, the weakest hummed along, others intoned praises to the glory of God at the top of their lungs, to forget their fate, reduce their suffering during sordid hours, in the absence of light, and to no longer think of the rape, the skulls of children crushed by blows from rifle butts. To pick up a dream or two of hope in the glimmer of the flames.

Louise Nzila passed on without tears. She rejoined the army of those gifted with death. Hundreds, thousands of innocent people fell into the field of the forgotten, due to misfortune or a random bullet fired by an annoyed militiaman barely fifteen years old. In the darkness of the civil war, life was worth nothing! A mouthful of dirty water that slowly kills!

Others perished from being beaten with clubs for giving an imprecise answer to an ignorant sergeant with issues, who had gotten up on the wrong side of the bed. Many gave up the ghost quietly in the humidity of the jungle. They lay down and rotted slowly without a cry or lamentation, much less funeral ceremonies, in the greatest indifference. These living-dead got used to the smells of putrefaction, walked without purpose, fed off the roots of the land, off the emptiness, and in the end collapsed a little farther along and departed for the invisible world where there is no more suffering and you are welcomed and consoled by regretful spirits. Love, love. Forever smiling, Mother Earth was silent!

As we paraded proudly through the apocalypse, the shadow of hate oozed from our gaze and stuck to our skin. Some misguided divinities had relegated the humanity in our hearts to the past. Novelty and difference were troubling, frightening, and destabilizing. With huge drops of sweat on their foreheads, they feared that we might not agree with them; we trampled on them, diminished them through humiliation or silence, at least for the time being. One or two liters of gasoline, a tire for a necklace, a spark, a blaze, a stone that crushes the skull.

~

Today, to survive on the ruins still smoking with the smells of destruction, men and women get drunk and seek refuge in bars and churches. Red-hot iron branded their bodies and souls. A permanent diurnal nightmare. Destiny has slipped from their hands. Many have given up.

CHRISTELLE NOW KNEW everything and maybe even more. I awaited sentencing in silence, feeling small. What was she going to do with my nakedness? After delivering myself to the judgment of a woman who was almost a stranger to me, I felt more destitute than ever.

She could open her arms to me, even wider than the night before, or reject me forever. I had revealed myself as I am without pretense. My honesty had lifted an enormous weight off my heart. I wanted her to accept me as the person I had become in her presence in this short time. I lowered my eyes, drained, as though I had just finished a race. Her silence all around me.

At the end of my story, pale, Christelle did not utter a word for some time. Her head was spinning rapidly; I could almost hear her thinking. A long sigh. Once again, her illusions had collapsed miserably into the ugliness of harsh reality. I hoped to have her mercy. My story had not brought me honor.

I would have loved to have told her that perhaps the secret of our story lay in the wisdom of taking what life had given to us now. We had been able to resuscitate the precious desire to love without holding back. Thanks to her presence and the color of her smiles, Christelle had taken me far away from the ashes of the past. She had the power to send me back.

～

Difficult still, for her to bear all of that. My story had exceeded any horror she could have imagined. Christelle could never have suspected that human beings were capable of such senseless acts. She had opened her heart to a monster, executioner and victim all in the same soul.

～

She still felt something for me, in spite of everything. Her hesitation betrayed her. At moments, while she looked at me, she immersed herself in the sensual feeling she had discovered with me, the impression that I was possibly indispensable to her happiness. Those honeymoon hours by my side thrilled her even more in this moment. She did not despise me. Christelle was sure of that now. I knew how to be true. She might have covered me with kisses to thank me for so much honesty, convinced that together we would succeed in decisively dispelling the shadow of Admiral Nzila Rambo and that I still had the strength to love.

～

When the monstrosity of my actions had appeared before her with such intolerable cruelty, Christelle hoped I was lying. She vacillated between tenderness and fear, and even surprised herself by invoking the goddess of whom I had spoken in my dream. Christelle also took refuge in Mother Earth. She imagined huge, wide-open legs, the same dimensions as the universe, a magisterial corolla, hot and humid, in whose depths we took shelter, intertwined together in the source of time, hopes, and dreams.

～

I ventured a trembling hand toward Christelle. Unlike our first night, this time it was she who nestled against my chest, teary-eyed, and mumbled:

"It's all over, Clovis, now you are here with me!"

Christelle sat up slowly and then invited me into her arms, to relieve me of my torment and allow me to start all over again.

Eyes closed, hesitating, she came close to me and offered her lips.

⌒

Still feeling awkward, I embraced her, shaking. She inhaled deeply to fill her lungs with my presence. Christelle quivered. A languorous wave moved gradually to the tips of her hair, through her veins and arteries. Slowly, she exhaled her final doubts. I understood when our eyes finally met as she brought me closer, there, on the floor, with poetry and fire in her eyes! We rolled around together awkwardly for a few seconds. The contorted waltz of passion searched for its path. We kissed with so much force, full on the mouth, that our teeth banged together. The shock of the parquet floor opened the dance, until we found the rhythm that soothes and intoxicates, at times fluid, brutal, and wild. Movements dreamed of a thousand times. The velvety and pungent taste of her skin.

Burning, sovereign ruler, she rose up, queen of our movements. Guided by desire and passion, Christelle accompanied me, all the while letting her desire brew. New reflections in our eyes, pupils dilated, drowning in tears of joy, reaching toward infinite vertiginous heights. She taught me how to caress, to be patient, and to go easy and then with intensity. She was the one who set off a torrent, a cascade, bites that sent us into writhing movements that kept coming and going. An uncontrollable torrid flow on our spicy tongues, which did not know how to stop, teeth clenching on my lower lip, taking me to the edge of what was bearable. Our fingers knotted together. Taste every inch of each other's bodies. Touch each other. More and more caresses that make us contort and forget ourselves. Murmurs, groans. Breathing in unison. Streams of perspiration to dress the skin, when words play with indecency and sweeten the madness. Not thinking about anything, at least not in this moment, imagined for seconds, hours, longed for and feared. Expansive feelings, outrageous pleasure, delicious fusion of bodies in convulsion, absence, feverish levitation. A thrilling embrace, eager and hungry, stronger, faster, always gentle!

Christelle held me tightly against her so that I would never leave! Then there was nothing but this powerful and magnificent luminosity, a prayer of cries and letting go. I exploded too. She was the first to fall asleep.

DURING THE NIGHT, in sleep flooded with pleasure, I glimpsed Marcelline, majestic, she appeared tenderly in my dream. At first somewhat vague, her image eventually became clearer and clearer. Light, happy, guided by Mother Earth, she came close to me and for the last time gave me her shoulder, on which I placed my cheek and a farewell kiss from the tip of my tongue. She smiled, relieved. Marcelline seemed to delight in my pleasure. She had been so afraid for me. Years had gone by, we had survived.

Freeing ourselves of yesterday, naked and purified of the errors and even the joys of bygone times. Marcelline had come to visit my spirit for the last time, certain that I had finally become who I had always wanted to be. Like two children taking off barefoot on the paths, we had returned to the beginning of the rupture and then soared.

It was the night of the solstice. Our bodies were bathed in light, surrounded by a gentle perfume; a new wind was blowing! It was with Christelle that I would now begin my mornings, days and nights of joy.

⌁

Marcelline and I gradually drew apart, glad for this final embrace. Love, love! It was she who whispered these final words. It's OK, Clovis; it's time to flow toward the pleasures and the forgotten. Marry and have a child!

CHRISTELLE AND I stayed for hours on the foldout sofa. We were savoring the luxury of loving each other tenderly and sensually. Our morning consisted of a succession of short, sweet kisses, eyes closed, and passionate embraces. She welcomed me several times into her moist universe. I set off gently into the joyful liquid.

Christelle, intoxicated and uninhibited, gave me the smooth curve of the small of her back, accentuated for even more pleasure. She forgot herself in the abyss, forestalling every restraint on my part when she held my pelvis forcefully against her own, her nails dug powerfully into my flesh. Out of breath, I let go one more time in her hair, soaked in red and silver and sighs, right up until that blessed moment when, stricken by pleasure, her body convulsed in fits. Christelle seemed to suffer for a second before letting go, a soft and supple dance, a stream of desires, which gradually ended in the calm of sleep. Alone in our paradise amid all that belongs to the city, we tasted harmony and peace. Christelle wanted time to stop so that the moment could be repeated infinitely. Lascivious and smiling, she covered me in kisses, stretched out, and said:

"What we need now is a good breakfast!"

I offered to go and get some fresh bread and warm croissants if she would point me in the right direction. In the meantime, she would make the coffee and prepare the table.

I got dressed with the help of Christelle, who handed me my clothes, joking, teasing me for my bad taste in fashion. Then she laughed, revealing a tender and mischievous pout. Her simple, funny way of celebrating good-bye created an enchanting atmosphere, and then I decided to leave.

I was reaching for the door handle when she leaped toward me and kissed me affectionately. She held me as though we were one body. I had the glimmer of her eyes, like a landscape, their sparkle hardly dimmed by her tears of joy. The green and black on the white background blended perfectly, a somber and luminous ode, a hymn of regrets and hopes. Her eyes expressed all the sadness and magic of our world, the two of us, our fears, our digressions, and the sudden promise of having met each other.

Her eyes half closed, Christelle was so close to me that I was enjoying her warm, irregular breath and getting light-headed, revived by the feel of her full breasts on my chest. An intensity of velvet softness of an unheard-of power, a sweet music, throbbing, sharp on the tip of her tongue.

"Hurry right back, I miss you already!"

I finally left the apartment and ran quickly down the stairs. I was sailing, floating somewhere toward the horizon. The clear, radiant sky dressed the ugliness of the beltway town with a beautiful azure blue dotted here and there with flakes soft, bright white clouds.

～

I crossed the interminable alley by the railway station as Christelle had told me to do. The road was practically deserted on this day of rest. I walked quickly, certain of my footing, humming a lullaby. I passed in front of the railroad station, the café, and the bus stops. I saw the place where we had met in full light. The events of the past hours came back to me. I was still distracted, joyful, replaying the sun-drenched, bright images. Still in a good mood, I headed to the bakery. I waited in line for a few minutes. When it was my turn, I stated my order politely and thanked the very pleasant baker lady.

On the way back, two patrol officers were checking a young man's ID in front of the train station. A dark blue CRS police van was parked about thirty feet away. I had to walk in front of it to get back to Christelle's. I hesitated a moment, painfully swallowing a ball of saliva before wiping my forehead several times, my gaze fixed on the ground and my head lowered. I was tempted to turn back, take off once again and hide. I thought about breakfast with Christelle, she and I relaxing in the smell of coffee and warm croissants. The image of Christelle, all smiles on the doorsteps, gave me courage, I imagined her opening the door and leaping into my arms.

Flooded with fear and anxiety, I hunched my back and lowered my eyes as I passed in front of the police. Severe, suspicious gazes pressed heavily on my back. One of the officers summoned me over, pointing his index finger in my direction and then bringing it back toward himself in an authoritarian manner. I pretended not to see him and hurried on. I heard:

"Police!"

The rest of the threat was masked by the terrifying silence of the wind being knocked out of me. My heart was suddenly beating wildly, as the blood rushed through my veins and almost exploded out of the pores of my skin, my knees gave way and started to tremble, a devastating thunderbolt in my head and fragments of forgotten prayers in my language. Salvation had crumbled away within seconds and disappeared. A moan lodged itself in my dry mouth. The mirage suddenly became blurry. My sky became cloudy. A concert of screams and commands to obey compelled me to take flight! It was all-out panic, run for your life, all at once. Meltdown, total confusion, everyone was suddenly on my tail, a crazy stampede going every which way, with no clear direction, desperate.

Hearing the ominous tread of boots, panic quickly replaced hysteria. I went up a random alley and found myself at a dead-end. I tried in vain to climb a wall, about two meters high, but came crashing down to the ground. I was bleeding. The dirty, black dust of the asphalt mixed with my blood. Dizzy from the fall, I managed to get up, however painfully, a few seconds later.

I heard the voices very close to me that would announce the tragic ending. My legs froze. Hope had failed at the foot of the wall. Despair imposed a cynical kaleidoscope in which I recognized the remains of my ancestors, militia comrades left behind to scavengers in the implacable sun and rain. A multitude of bodies was floating in the river or rotting in the jungle. I caught a glimpse of Marcelline's suffering and Christelle's face in a terrible grimace of distress.

～

My knees, injured from the concrete after the violent truncheon blows to my back and head, brought me back to reality, unbearable misery. Some seconds later, I was eating dust again, my lip cracked and my nose broken. Several CRS officers then brutally pulled me up from the ground and threw my body against the concrete. I briefly glimpsed the bread and croissants being trampled. They were bathing in the mud. Despite the insults, I held on to my dignity and refused to answer their questions. They used the official terms prescribed by procedure. I especially heard resentment, incomprehension, sadness, and contempt.

I thought of begging them to let me go back to Christelle, to speak with her one last time. But behind the lowered visors, there was not one ounce of humanity or spark of compassion. There was only coldness, order, and hate. I was invisible! A trivial object, a duty to be accomplished, a law to be applied, with the mission being to bring it to a successful conclusion with maximum efficiency and the least possible damage. Upright, firm, and deaf, they systematically beat and trampled on me. I was engulfed in a rancid tide in my throat, my belly, and my chest.

~

Christelle would remain for hours, perhaps days, weeks, or months, waiting for me, her beautiful green eyes inundated with acid, bitter tears. Her features swollen once more due to misfortune, nerves frayed, fingers clenched, nails forever scratching purplish wounds of solitude and deception.

~

I was pushed forcibly into the armored car. I prayed quietly to Mother Earth to protect Christelle and console her during the tortures of absence. They secured me to a metal bench in the van and then closed the door firmly. In a moment of lucidity, I countered the sudden jolt of the van taking off with a solid push to the left to avoid falling backward. My hands bound, I clenched my fists. Rage swelled up inside me all the way to my throat and once again revived the strength to resist . . . Survive at all costs!

Indestructible despite my swollen face and the wounds in my soul, I nourished myself on Marcelline's love, on Christelle's tenderness, on the honeymoon hours and the peace I had found. Not to mention our crazy desires in the depths of her belly, suspended for a brilliant tomorrow.

The van was taking me far away, away from hope, away from the vertiginous fever of her body.

This night, alone on the edge of madness, Christelle, stomach knotted and tears pouring down, will not sleep!

~

The implausible had loaned me wings for two nights, a beacon in the darkness, a mirage, an inspiration of red curls on bare shoulders, a dream of a green gaze, rest and ecstasy on warm skin. Magic, the craziness, to believe in the unbelievable.

My momentary flight had wound up broken, annihilated by contact with steel and the law! I continue to wander, heading nowhere, cooped up like an animal, bitterness in my heart, dreams in shreds.

WILFRIED N'SONDÉ was born in 1969 in Brazzaville, Democratic Republic of the Congo, and grew up in France. He is widely considered one of the shining lights of the new generation of African and Afropean writers. His work has received considerable critical attention and been recognized with prestigious literary awards, including the Prix des Cinq Continents de la Francophonie and the Prix Senghor de la création littéraire.

KAREN LINDO is a scholar of French and Francophone literatures and currently teaches and translates in Paris.

DOMINIC THOMAS has published numerous books and edited volumes on the cultural, political, and social relations between Africa and France and on immigration and race in Europe, including *Black France* (IUP, 2007) and *Africa and France* (IUP, 2013). He has translated works by Aimé Césaire, Faïza Guène, Alain Mabanckou, and Abdourahman A. Waberi. He is the Global African Voices series editor at Indiana University Press.

CPSIA information can be obtained
at www.ICGtesting.com
Printed in the USA
FSOW01n2210080817
37379FS